W9-CRI-145

What She Missed

LIARA TAMANI

What
She Missed

GREENWILLOW BOOKS
AN IMPRINT OF HarperCollins Publishers

What She Missed
Copyright © 2023 by Liara Tamani

The text of this book is set in Garamond 3 LT Std.
Book design by Sylvie Le Floc'h

Library of Congress Cataloging-in-Publication Data

Names: Tamani, Liara, author.
Title: What she missed / by Liara Tamani.
Description: First edition. | New York : Greenwillow Books, an imprint of HarperCollins Publishers, 2023. | Audience: Ages 13 up. | Audience: Grades 7-9. | Summary: Sixteen-year-old Ebony is devastated when her family moves from Houston to her grandmother's house in the country, but in her new small Texas town, she pushes her boundaries until she realizes she may have gone too far.
Identifiers: LCCN 2022062176 (print) | LCCN 2022062177 (ebook) | ISBN 9780063093287 (hardcover) | ISBN 9780063093300 (ebook)
Subjects: CYAC: Family life—Fiction. | Friendship—Fiction. | Love—Fiction. | African Americans—Fiction. | Texas—Fiction.
Classification: LCC PZ7.1.T355 Wh 2023 (print) | LCC PZ7.1.T355 (ebook) | DDC [Fic]—dc23
LC record available at https://lccn.loc.gov/2022062176
LC ebook record available at https://lccn.loc.gov/2022062177

23 24 25 26 27 LBC 5 4 3 2 1
First Edition
Greenwillow Books

For Amina and young readers everywhere

Don't be afraid of the unknown.
As you grow and change,
stay close to the things you love,
the things that bring you light and joy and peace.
In time, more will be revealed.

What
She
Missed

Wrong way. Written in all caps on a red-and-white sign. Ebony sped right by it after she took a left at Stevie's Boat Rental. A turn too soon. She wasn't paying attention.

A hard blow to the face. She didn't know what it was until the airbag started to deflate. She'd hit something. Or worse, someone.

Everything around her grew sharp. Clear. The high, continuous note in her ears. The blood running out of her nose and dripping from her lips. The metallic taste of it, tinged with strawberry-flavored gloss. The cracked windshield streaked red. The headlight beams on the pitch-black road ahead.

Ebony stared at the blood, wondering how she'd been

so blind. Her life wasn't over. She still had so much to discover . . . to create . . . to celebrate . . . to love . . . so much to lose.

Why hadn't she known that?

Well, she had, but then she forgot. It was crazy how hard it was to keep track of herself. How she could learn something about herself and then forget. Learn it again and think she'd learned something new.

But that night would never leave her. In a flash, it would summon all the scattered moments of the summer that had led her there. Every struggle. Every wild and stupid thing she'd done. The love she was afraid to feel. Every wrong turn.

Chapter
1

I wanted to go home.

I thought about opening the back door of Daddy's pickup truck and jumping out. But at that point, I still had good sense. We were on a highway, not a country road. It was real life, not a movie. I could die, paralyze myself, or get mangled by the U-Haul.

And I still liked myself too much to risk any of that. Well, most of myself. The percentage could fluctuate on any given day. But I liked the way my name matched my dark skin, which complimented any color eyeliner I wore. I liked the way the small gap between my two front teeth made me feel extra cute, especially on days I rocked mismatched prints. I liked my big lips and strong legs. And don't even get me started on how long I'd grown out my chunky twists. Or the way I signed my name: the *s* of *Jones* dramatically traveling off the canvas.

I thought about screaming, *You're ruining my life!* at the top of my lungs. But I knew that wouldn't change anything and only make me feel pathetic. Plus, I didn't want to hear another one of Mom's speeches about being positive. She was big on being positive, and it made me sick.

So I just sat there, staring out of the window. Watching miles and miles of nothing go by. No museums or art galleries, no strangers walking by or riding bikes, no ice cream or vintage T-shirt shops, no Chinese spot down the block with the most delicious barbeque bao on earth. Only land and sky. And the June Texas sun glaring at me as it blazed high in the blue, beating down anything out in the open. Killing everything soft.

"Windmill!" shouted Mom, pointing to a wooden tower in a field of yellow grass. "That's twelve."

"Twelve is nothing," Daddy responded.

"It's one more than you," Mom popped back.

I wasn't playing, but I still felt like I was in last place. Twelve to eleven to none.

I imagined myself walking out into the yellow grass

and igniting—painted flames shooting from my shoulders, engulfing my head.

I imagined my funeral. Everyone sad and dressed in black. My parents wishing they never would've sold our house and made me leave Houston. Justine, Dani, and Cara wishing they wouldn't have dragged me to the mall my last day there. Knowing I was broke. Knowing I was lying when I said I couldn't find anything cute or that I didn't want a cinnamon sugar pretzel from Annie's. And Miles wishing he would've kissed me while he had the chance.

Can you tell me how a perfect love goes wrong?
Can somebody tell me how to get things back
The way they use to be?

Daddy's voice strained over Boyz II Men as he sang in Mom's direction. He was always singing along to some old-school R & B song, but this was one of Mom's favorites.

Mom took a break from the hunt and smiled at him.

"Windmill! Windmill!" Daddy shouted, and he pointed to two rusted metal towers on adjoining hills.

"Ooh, you dirty!"

Daddy admitted nothing. Only rubbed his short beard and laughed and laughed.

The two of them really got on my nerves sometimes. The way their love seemed to be able to go anywhere, despite anything. It wasn't like I wanted them to scream and fight like Dani's parents. But they'd lost a lot, too. I didn't get them.

Especially Mom. I could count on one hand the number of times she'd been to Gigi's lake house. Having grown up in a high-rise in Houston's Galleria area, she was not about that country life. Too quiet, she'd always said. But there she was in a straw bolero hat and a sleeveless denim button up, playing the part.

"Windmill!" they said at the same time and proceeded to argue about whose lips the *w* came off first.

"Would you *please* shut the fuck up?" I said under my breath.

The fire in me turned cold. *I didn't mean it. It's just a phrase I picked up at school*, I prepared to lie.

No whips of necks or breaks in debate, and I realized my parents didn't hear. But even if they had, the way I saw it (safely, in retrospect) was that my parents having so much fun was a cruel affront to the loss I was experiencing.

I tuned them out and tried to remember how close

Miles's lips came to mine the second-to-last day of school. I tried to remember the way he smelled. Like emerald-green trees. Like sunshine and paint. Like something else, but I couldn't remember. Only three hours outside Houston, and he was already slipping away.

High stone walls on either side of the car—the road cutting through solid rock. And for a second, I was my great-great-grandmother, crossing the passage into safety. Gigi's old story surprised me. So familiar but unfamiliar. Like a movie I'd forgotten most of the parts to.

But I was remembering.

We were close. Another mile or so before the fork in the road, a right toward the southern part of the lake, ten minutes of old highway cutting through dry, rocky earth and tree-covered hills, a left at the fruit stand, a climb up a hill so steep you can only see sky, back down eyeing asphalt, and a few more turns past small wooden houses before Daddy's tires would crunch over gravel up the final hill to Gigi's house.

What
She
Missed

A bouquet of ten black balloons. Caught high between two big branches of an oak tree in front of the fruit stand. Floated over from a wake down the street. Lost but not lost. There for them and then there for her. To mourn. To celebrate. But she didn't see the long, black strings, bound together, waving at her in the wind.

Chapter 2

*G*igi's house was just as I remembered. A light-green bungalow with deep-green shutters, surrounded by white rock, weeds, and trees. As I stepped out of the truck, I paused. Waiting for the screen door to open . . . waiting for Gigi to walk out onto the porch in one of her off-the-shoulder muumuus . . . waiting to feel the warmth of her welcome.

Gigi is dead, I reminded myself. *And this is not Gigi's house anymore. Clearly.*

Three wicker lounge chairs from our backyard in Houston were already sitting in the southwest corner of the porch, facing the lake down below. The hanging plants that used to drape over the railing were gone. The potted plants and giant crystals that lined the three steps leading up to the porch were gone. The tear in the bottom left corner of the screen door (where my six-year-old self accidentally kicked it in) was gone, too.

And where was the wind chime? The golden bells that hung from the porch's east side? Gigi used to say they made the sound of the God.

My phone vibrated on the backseat, and I reached inside the truck to grab it. A group text from Justine: *Please tell us you've opened it.*

Dani added a GIF of Regina Hall anxiously eating a bowl of popcorn.

Cara texted a cat scratching at a door. She was the worst at GIFs.

The three of them wouldn't let me get that envelope out of my mind. The one I'd found in my art bin after I'd gotten home from the mall. Crisp and red with "Ebony" written in the center in Miles's neat, cursive handwriting. He must've snuck it in on the last day of school.

But I couldn't bring myself to open it. I figured that having a confirmation of how much Miles liked me . . . of how much he'd miss me . . . in his own words . . . would only make me more pissed that he didn't kiss me.

I climbed back in the truck, away from the sun, and

searched for a responding GIF. A man shoveling dirt over a grave. A baller making a cutting motion to his throat mouthing, "Game over." A woman in sunglasses throwing her hand in somebody's face, the words "Stop it" underneath.

But before I could choose, the other back door opened and Mom's soft arms were lifting two bags out of the backseat. "Indigo, can you help bring in some of these groceries? They've been out of the fridge long enough."

"It's Eb-on-y," I corrected her, emphasizing every syllable of my name.

"Sorry," she replied, and carried the bags toward the house.

I shoved my phone in the front pocket of my jean shorts. It hadn't been that long since I'd changed my name back, I knew that. But I still couldn't help getting heated over Mom's slipups.

See, a year earlier, I'd changed my name to Indigo. The genius thing about it was that Indigo was still a color. A color that better represented who I was. For exactly ten months, three weeks, and five days.

I'd tried to save face by waiting to change my name back to Ebony, the name my parents gave me, as long as I possibly could. Until hearing "Indigo" made me want to take a two-by-four from one of the building sites Daddy used to supervise and smash the word with it—deep-blue and violet splatters everywhere.

But waiting hadn't saved me from feeling ridiculous. And I was sure Mom called me Indigo from time to time just to make me feel stupid all over again.

When I stepped into the house, I thought I smelled the incense Gigi always burned. But when I took another breath, it wasn't there. The only thing of Gigi's in the room was one of the ten-foot plant-dyed canvases she used to sell to boutiques in Austin. It was hanging behind the sofa, unstretched—Sam Gilliam–style—covered in faded blues and purples. I walked over to it and ran the tip of my nose across its edge to see if I could smell elderberries or hyacinth or woad. Nothing.

"In here," Mom called out.

I hated how she acted like she hadn't sent me to stay there every summer of my childhood while she traveled for work. "I'm pretty sure I know where the kitchen is, Mom."

"Ebony," Daddy sang softly, walking past carrying two duffle bags toward the hall. He always played referee.

I dropped the groceries off on the kitchen counter, ran a hand over its scalloped teal tile, and headed to my room before Mom could ask me to do anything else.

Daddy had been going back and forth to get the house ready for weeks, but I'd told him to leave my old room alone. The plain white comforter and pillows. The polished cherry oak wardrobe with an oval mirror on the front. Paintings by my younger self, framed and hung gallery-style on the white walls. Colorful strokes so filled with joy they felt foreign.

I picked up a pillow and brought it to my nose. Hoping to smell rosewater or incense or bacon or smoke.

Again, nothing.

Then I turned and saw the picture of me and my friends on the nightstand. I'd left the photo in the bottom drawer of my old dresser, hoping it would get lost in storage. But I guess Daddy had found it and framed it.

We were sitting on the school lawn the Friday before spring break. Dani was holding a piece of popcorn up to the sky like a champagne glass. She was blurry but smiling. Justine was palming the bottom of the buttery bag. Her lips were barely closed over her full mouth. Cara had her tongue out and her eyes closed. Her right elbow, hanging over her thigh, was ashy. She was leaning on me. My head was tilted. My bra straps were showing. And I was looking straight at the camera mid-laugh.

That was happiness. And it was all about to get snatched away from me. But in the picture, I didn't know it yet.

My right hip vibrated. Another group text from Dani: *Well?*

Just leave it alone, I responded. Jealous they'd get to stay together. Mad they'd get to hang out all summer and go back to Houston's Academy of the Arts in the fall while I was stuck in the boonies.

I tossed my phone on the bed and headed out back to Gigi's old studio: a converted garage with glass doors and a row of windows running along the sides and back. In front of it, the big black cauldron Gigi used to dye her canvases in wasn't over the fire pit. Now there were only half-burned branches sticking up out of ashes.

It was hot inside, but I didn't bother trying to find the remote control for the air-conditioning unit above the door. My paintings hung on walls, sat on shelves, and were propped up against buckets and stools. Gigi's huge canvases covered the ceiling. Her crystals and rock formations (spirals, lines, and stacks) were spread out on tables with her books and ceramic pots. My paintbrushes, colored pencils, and markers waved hello to me from Gigi's mason jars. My paint tubes seemed to be saying *whee* as they dangled upside down in the air—their ends squeezed by binder clips, which hung from a row of nails halfway hammered into the wood-planked walls.

I heard a tinkling sound coming from the back corner of the studio and walked toward it. *The golden bells!* I thought, seeing them hanging outside the window. Daddy had somehow gathered me and Gigi together in the same light-filled space and reminded me of how art could make me feel like I was everything.

Until I spotted my self-portrait on the easel under the back windows and felt like nothing. I starred at the blue-black blotch I'd painted over my face until my eyes welled up. Then I ran out of the studio and tried to forget about it.

Chapter 3

*W*hen I woke the next morning, my room was gray—sun almost completely blocked by the dark-green curtains. Despite the gap in the middle of the drapery, where light crept through, the room mostly matched the cloud I saw hanging over my future. And I was glad to feel like something finally understood my misery.

Until, in the corner of the room, I saw two rainbow lines on the edge of the wardrobe mirror, where the glass was beveled. They almost touched but didn't. I moved my head this way and that, hoping to make them disappear, but the colors only changed from hot blues and greens to reds and yellows to indigos and violets.

When I realized I was playing with light, I stopped.

A few minutes later, there was a knock at my door.

"Yeah?" I moaned.

"There's someone here to see you." Mom's voice was muffled.

The only person it could've been was Jalen, my best friend from way back who lived in the house next door. Growing up, summers were an endless cycle of us playing together along the rocky shoreline of the lake and swimming together to cool down. But I hadn't seen him since Gigi died six years ago. An eternity.

And yet when I walked down the hall toward the kitchen and saw Jalen standing in front of the sink, talking to Daddy, he looked the same: tall and lanky with a goofy grin and an even goofier-looking bucket hat. Same light blue as his old hat with the same elastic drawstring that hung down around his chin. Same type of plain white T and faded swim trunks.

I wondered how he could stay the same all these years when I was constantly tweaking myself. My clothes, the way I wore my makeup, even my name. His sameness felt disorienting. It took me back to being in the kitchen with him and Gigi. At the table eating bacon and grapes (what Gigi called a light breakfast) before we all went down to the lake. Hungry and ready for biscuits, grits, and catfish after we came back. Making grilled cheese sandwiches on days Gigi disappeared into her studio.

As soon as Jalen spotted me, he clapped his hands together, screeched with glee, and high-stepped across the kitchen. "Ebony!" he exclaimed in a voice with more bass than I expected, and wrapped his arms around me.

"Jalen," I said, half-happy to see him and half-over-whelmed by how happy he was to see me. His brightness was a lot for me that morning. It made me want to duck off to find shade.

"About time!" he said, and let me go.

"You have a mustache," I replied, and stroked his short hairs with my pointer finger.

Smiling, he swatted my hand away like a fly. "Do you know how long I've been waiting for you to come back?"

"And hair on your chin." It made me wish I had boobs— big, bouncy boobs—to show off. But I still had little apricots.

"I'm serious, Ebony! Every summer I hoped you'd be back. Every time I saw your dad's truck parked in the drive-way, I hoped you'd be with him. But you never were. And now you're here for good."

"Yeah, unfortunately," I said, staring at the new angles in

his face, betting they had all the girls around town thinking he was fine.

The corners of his eyes shifted from excitement into something softer. "Dang, I didn't know Alula Lake was that bad."

"It's not," I replied, hoping I hadn't hurt his feelings. "It's just . . . well, a lot. But you know I'm happy to see you."

"You better be!" he said, widening his eyes.

"See, that's one of the things I love about real friendship," Mom said, holding a mug with a tea tag hanging over its side. She was sitting at the oval wooden table in her workout clothes and a hat to cover her hair. "You can always pick it up exactly where it left off."

Mom loved using clichés on me. I tried my best not to roll my eyes before walking past Jalen to get some orange juice out of the fridge. "Want some?" I asked, holding up the carton.

"Yes, please," he answered.

I opened the top cabinet, closest to the fridge, where Gigi kept the glasses. But it was full of plates.

"Next one," Mom said.

"You'll have to get Ebony out there," Daddy said as Jalen went back to stand near him.

"What's that?" Jalen asked

"Sailing."

"Oh, yeah. For sure," Jalen replied.

As I approached Jalen with the orange juice, he studied my face. But it didn't make me self-conscious like it usually did when I felt eyes on me. I offered him one of the glasses, and when he reached for it, I pulled it away. I did this a few times, trying to be funny.

Finally he snatched the glass and a strange, shiny thing pulled at the corners of my mouth. A real smile. I hadn't felt one in weeks. Juice pooled in the webbed skin between my thumb and pointer finger, and I licked it clean.

"Really, Ebony?" Mom said behind me.

Hearing the look of disgust on her face, I happily licked the juice dripping down the side of the glass, too.

"We were just talking about how Jalen took me sailing last week," Daddy continued.

Jalen turned toward Daddy. "Man, am I glad you were with me that day. The wind was crazy strong. I had to get you all the way out on the trapeze."

Daddy laughed. "Hadn't done that since I was a young buck. I was struggling."

Jalen laughed, too. "You were fine. Until the wind let up and you almost got dunked!"

"But I didn't. You had it all under control, Captain."

Hearing "Captain" made Jalen feel good. Embarrassingly good. He was too brown to turn red, but I could tell by the way he took an extra-long sip of his juice to hide his beaming face.

"I'll pass on getting dunked," I said, mostly to give Jalen a distraction.

"We can take a bigger boat out. Just wait, you're gonna love it," Jalen replied. And then, "Hey, wanna come down to the lake with me? Not to sail, just to hang for a bit. It's Thursday so I only have one swim lesson today. This kid named Alexander. He's improved a ton over the last couple of months. When he first came to me, he was still afraid to put his head under the water. Now he can swim almost halfway to the lighthouse. Anyway, I won't be tied up for too long. And I'm not due at Stevie's until one."

I didn't want to see the lake, but I liked the way Jalen was telling me a whole bunch of stuff I didn't need to know. The way it reminded me of what once was and made me wonder about what I'd missed. And I wanted to get away from my parents and press into all of it.

Chapter 4

I grabbed my old black Converse near the front door, shook them out for scorpions, and followed Jalen outside. As soon as our sneakers stepped off the porch and onto the crushed white rock, Jalen yelled, "Race ya!"

Same thing he used to say every summer morning when we were growing up, so I was ready.

I took off down the hill and he peeled after me. We hurdled the small boulders between our two properties, almost side by side.

"You really think you can still beat me, don't you?" he yelled, flashing me a smile.

Growing up, I beat Jalen all the time, but I couldn't remember the last time I'd raced anyone. I didn't even run unless I was late to class, trying to get away from a bee, or chasing somebody for putting ice down my shirt or something. But still I said, "Think? I know," partly because it felt good talking noise and partly because I was delusional.

He laughed. "Yeah, okay."

I wanted to say, *Keep laughing. You'll see,* but decided to save my breath. The lake was about a mile down the hill.

Jalen was ahead of me going into the woods. A good thing, because it had been awhile since I'd traveled through the trees—mostly live oaks, red oaks, and junipers—and I'd forgotten where their big roots surfaced along the path. Where the deep dips were in the earth. The big rocks. The low-hanging limbs.

I kept up for the first couple of minutes, but then I started to fall behind.

When Jalen looked back and saw that I was dragging, he slowed down to a gentler pace.

Still, my lungs burned. And even with the green leaves shielding us from the sun, I was sweating like crazy. I wanted to stop. I wanted to be the kind of person who didn't care about giving up. But I wasn't. So I kept running.

A minute later a screeching hawk flew off a branch and crossed right in front of Jalen's face. He stopped, turned around, and yelled, "Did you see that?"

It felt like the forest giving me a hand, and I sped up and tried to pass him.

"Oh, I see how it is. Let me stop playing with you." He took off, ducking below a tree's low arm.

I ducked, too, but not low enough, and one of the twists in my high bun got caught on a twig. "Ouch," I yelled as the tree yanked a few stands.

"Losing hurts, doesn't it?" he shouted over his shoulder.

"Shut up!"

We ran faster and my lungs felt like they were literally going to combust, but I was happier than I could remember being in months.

Finally the trees thinned out and I saw snatches of blue. With each step, the yellow grass got taller and the rocks larger until the rugged earth dropped down toward the beach. My feet surprised me. They still knew exactly where to step—which big rock most easily led down to the next and the next.

Taking the last hop down, I looked out at the lake— so sparkling blue it made me squint, so big it seemed to stretch out under the whole sky. I'd half hoped it would look janky—destroyed by all the new people moving here from

Austin and San Antonio that Daddy talked about. But it didn't. Even the old lighthouse, about a half a mile out along the south shore, gleamed.

Ahead of me, Jalen threw his T-shirt, hat, and sneakers onto the rocks and slammed into the water, high step after high step, and then dove in. Seconds passed and he popped up, smiling at me with a joy so pure it was sickening. Except that I desperately wanted to feel it myself. I didn't want to keep being sad about my life or pissed at my parents. I didn't want to keep fearing my future or being jealous of my friends. I wanted to feel happy to be alive again.

I ran toward Jalen until the lake's waves were breaking at the tips of my dirty Converse. Then I stopped and backed away.

"Ebony!" Jalen hollered, and waved at me to come in.

But I plopped down at the edge of the clear water. I knew I didn't want to see the lake; but it wasn't until I was up close, staring at it foaming at the mouth, that I realized how much I hated it. Mostly because I still loved it. After all those years of trying to forget about the lake—about this place—I could still feel traces of it inside me longing to return home.

"Come on! What are you doing?" yelled Jalen.

Sitting on the beach, hot and sweaty, with sharp rocks

and shells poking me in the butt, I imagined what it would be like to dive in. To swim and play with Jalen again. But there was no way. Gigi had given so much of her life to the lake. Swam in it every day. Taught children to backstroke and breaststroke and freestyle in it—to love it as she had. And it killed her anyway.

What
She
Missed

The cool water rushing up over her skin. Enveloping her. Moving through her hair and fingers as she swam.

Floating with her eyes closed, the sun a warm blanket and the water a cool bed.

A big splash—Jalen disturbing her peace.

Laughing and splashing him back.

Every playful exchange, every unchanged thing between them.

Gigi smiling down on all of it.

Chapter 5

My parents are liars. They told me anything was possible. They said if I worked hard enough that I could create the life I wanted for myself. They said all I had to do was paint the sky with my dreams and reach and reach and reach. And I was stupid enough to believe them.

That's what was going through my head the following Monday as I sat cross-legged in bed, retwisting my freshly washed hair and rereading Mr. Marshall's email over and over again.

Hi, Ebony,

You're one of the best students I've ever had, and I mean that. Change can be difficult, but please remember how talented you are. Why didn't you turn in your self-portrait? I'll give you an Incomplete for now, but that will change to an F if you don't submit it. Remember, your self-portrait is 40% of your final grade.

What happened to the last piece you were working on? I thought it was a great start. Feel free to begin again, but I'm not sure how much good it's doing you. Either way, I must have your self-portrait before August 15th. That's the last date to change the grade in the system. You can do this, Ebony. I know you can.

Best,
Mr. Marshall

I stopped twisting my hair and tossed my phone on the bed. Then I laid down on my back in the darkness, cursing myself for trying so hard in the first place.

I'd spent years working on my portfolio just to apply to Houston's Academy of the Arts. It was one of the top art high schools in the country, and I'd dreamed of graduating from there since I was eleven. Even after I got accepted, scared I wasn't good enough, I painted constantly the summer before my freshman year. With gouache, pastel, watercolor, and oil. I worked to get better at everything.

And when I got to my new school and my classmates and teachers admired my work, it made my dreams get bigger. Travel further. Like parts of me had already made it as a world-famous painter and were waiting for the rest of me to catch up. So I kept working and reaching, and after almost two years there, I beyond believed in myself. I loved the art I was creating so much that I couldn't see anything getting in the way of my future.

Then my parents took me to my favorite pizza spot and broke the news.

I was midbite of a slice of veggie when Mom said, "We're moving to Alula Lake."

"Huh?" I said, mouth full, sure I'd heard her wrong. I hadn't been back to the lake in forever. I didn't even like thinking about the place.

"I know it's a big change," Daddy continued, his thick hand cupped above his wild brows. He was sitting across from me at the table on a patio dotted with red-and-white checkered umbrellas that did little to block the sun. "But we've decided Alula Lake is best for us. You'll have to trust that we've thought long and hard—"

"But I don't want to spend my whole summer out

there," I whined, choosing to believe he was talking about something temporary even though Mom had lost her job as a senior management consultant six months prior. Even though I knew the money Daddy brought in as the superintendent of a home building company wasn't enough to pay all the bills. "Can't I just stay here with Justine? Please? Y'all know her parents won't mind."

I imagined spending the summer alternating between playing with Justine's one-legged cat, Devonte, and going to paint at Miles's house, which was only one hundred and eighty-eight steps away (Justine, me, Cara, and Dani had counted one night at a sleepover). Thinking about it made the sun feel like a loving arm around my shoulders. I tilted my slice of pizza to wrangle in a wandering olive and took another bite.

"Not for the summer, Ebony," Mom replied, her voice going firm. "We're moving to Alula Lake for good."

The sky melted into the umbrellas. A red, white, and blue blur. The sun, a hundred degrees hotter on the back of my neck, made my throat feel like it was packed with dust.

Daddy cut Mom a look and then started going on about fresh starts and new opportunities. But his words got lost in the blur, now swirling with the lake and Gigi's dead body and my art school and friends.

"But I can't move! My life is here!" I'd wanted to scream the words at the top of my lungs, but they'd barely made it out of my hot, dusty throat.

Daddy gently explained that moving wasn't an option. He'd lost his job two months prior. They didn't tell me because they didn't want me to worry. But they'd put our house on the market earlier that week.

Something inside me cracked. Shifted. It was in that moment I realized that life could change in an instant. That everything I loved, everything I worked for, could be ripped away from me. That I'd had no control over anything.

So, what's the point, Mr. Marshall? I screamed silently, rolling over onto my side. *What's the point of working so hard? Of doing this stupid, impossible self-portrait when none of it will matter in the end?*

I had been there many times over the last couple of months—lying on my bed, in the dark, on the verge of tears—and knew exactly where things were headed. A disgustingly snotty pillow. A wastebasket full of tissues I'd have to empty into a grocery bag and hide in the trash. Swollen eyes I'd have to ice back to normal in the morning.

I started to curl myself up into a tight ball for a long cry but stopped. I told myself back in Houston that there would be no more of that.

I needed to get out of the house.

I reached for my phone and, squinting into its brightness, texted Jalen.

Chapter 6

*W*ith my phone's flashlight shining down on the broken stems, leaves, rocks, and roots, I walked next door through the woods. A short distance, but it had been awhile since I'd walked through trees at night, and I was glad when I made it to Jalen's driveway.

He was sitting on a beach chair in the bed of an old, red pickup with another chair beside him. "Hey," he said as I approached the truck. Then he stood up and held out his hand.

"I'm good," I said, kicking off my cheetah slides. I swung one leg onto the tailgate and pushed myself up. I'd had plenty of practice getting onto the back of Daddy's truck. But the beach chair was new for me. It was lower than I expected it to be, and when I went to sit, I plopped down so hard I almost tipped over.

"You okay?"

"No, my teacher is trying to give me an F," I said, moving past my clumsiness.

"Damn, that's no good."

"Not at all. I hate that man," I huffed, wanting to feel Jalen on my side. But I actually loved Mr. Marshall. The way he always encouraged his students to experiment and develop our own styles. He was by far my favorite teacher. I was just pissed at him for making me do something I found impossible. "He's such a dick."

"What class is it?"

"Painting."

"What? But that's always been your thing! You know I still have all the watercolors you did of me hanging up in my room, right?"

"No, you do not!"

"Well, you said I'd better keep them because they'd be worth millions one day when you got world famous."

I laughed. "Boy, I was ten!"

"So! Kids be doing it big these days. Wait, don't tell me you've fallen off. I still have a drawer full of all the other paintings you gave me, too. And I'm trying to get paid."

"Whatever."

"I'm serious! I got boats to buy!"

"Boats? What boats?"

"All the boats!" he said and laughed. But then he got serious. "No, but really I'm trying to buy a sailboat. Not the dinghy I took your dad out on. A big one. And when I get more money, I wanna trade up for a bigger boat. And then a bigger boat. Basically, keep trading up until I finally get *the* boat."

"Wait a minute. Don't tell me you're still trying to sail the world?" He'd been talking about it since we were kids.

"Hell, yeah! I'm *going to* sail the world! All I have to do is keep upgrading until I get a boat big and bad enough to handle the high seas."

Jalen spoke with so much confidence that he made his dream sound inevitable. Like it was just a matter of time. And I missed thinking that way. The hope it gave to life.

"You'll have to meet me in Paris or Florence or Cape Town . . . wherever I'll be," I said, getting in on the dream game. Before my life got all messed up, I'd imagined having exhibits in museums and shows around the world by age twenty-five.

"Bet. I'll have to make stops anyway. You can show me around whatever city you're living in."

"Yeah, and take you to whatever gallery my work—"

Behind Jalen, a girl appeared in the porch light.

"Dang, Jalen!" I said, staring at her walking toward us. At her reddish-brown buzz cut almost the same color of her rich, brown skin. At the thick black choker around her neck. The other long black necklace tied at the center of her collarbones, with green stones dangling on its ends. Her small breasts, free from a bra, in her tan tank with spaghetti straps.

"What?"

"Why didn't you tell me you had company?"

Jalen turned to look over his left shoulder. "Company? Nah, that's Lena."

"That's Lena?" I asked in disbelief. Lena was Jalen's half sister. A year older. She'd always stayed the summers with her mom in North Carolina, so I'd never met her. Only heard about her. Usually, the trouble she was getting in.

Nobody ever told me she was so beautiful. Or that she'd be here this summer. As she approached, I took in as much of her as I could. The small cursive tattoo on her right shoulder. The other one on her right side, peeking out from her cropped tank top. The tiny silver hoop in her left nostril. Her nude lipstick, a few shades darker than her bare, smooth skin.

Just looking at her made me feel insecure, which made me want to get closer to her. To absorb some of what she was, to know some of what she knew. There seemed to be so much there to explore, to mimic, to try on.

Lena stopped in front of the truck. "So you're Ebony," she said, looking me over like I was a preview to a show that she was trying to decide whether to watch.

The pink starry jumpsuit I had on suddenly felt stupid. I'd known it was risky when I saw it in T.J. Maxx a few weeks earlier. On the fine line between bold and doing way too much. But I liked it and when Mom had said I could get it, I'd quickly decided it was the perfect kind of bold. *Wrong!* And my hair. I'd only finished half of my twists. The other half was still up in a scrunchie. I was so embarrassed. "Actually, it's Indigo now. Ebony was my name growing up."

"Indigo?" Jalen asked, making a face.

"I didn't want to make a big deal out of it, but yeah." A lie, obviously. The reflex of changing my name again had surprised even me, but in that moment it felt necessary. And not just because I was trying to impress Lena.

A year before I'd felt really drawn to the name Indigo. I never got why, entirely, but I couldn't ignore the attraction.

It was like "Indigo" was some kind of mystery I needed to understand. Until I found out I was moving, decided the name was impossible and stupid, and changed it back.

But after that, I never felt right. It's like I was stuck—suspended between my old self, which was fading, and my new self, who wasn't formed yet. Anyway, using "Indigo" again now with Lena seemed to propel me forward, out of limbo. Toward what? I didn't know. But it felt like a beginning. A spark.

"All right then. I'm out," Lena said to Jalen, seemingly uninterested in my name drama.

"You going to The Cove?" he asked her.

"Yeah."

"Again?"

"Yeah."

"Another party?"

"I guess."

"His parents don't care?"

"They're in Austin."

"For how long?"

"Most of the summer, I think. They go back and forth. But from the sound of it, they mainly spend their time there."

Jalen leaned forward in his chair. "What? Why rent out

all of The Cove, then? They must have some serious cash to burn."

Lena pulled her phone from the back pocket of her frayed jean shorts and started texting. "Yeah, his mom invented some kind of encryption software. And they're not renting it."

"What do you mean?"

"It's theirs. They bought it."

"What? When did the McLearys sell their property?" Jalen asked, sounding hurt.

"Look," Lena said, still staring down at her phone. "I don't have all the answers."

"Well, you've been up there every night for almost a week."

She whipped her head up. "And? You ain't Daddy."

"Yeah, but you know good and well he said that just because he's working the night shift doesn't mean—"

"Anyway," she interrupted him, and turned toward a car pulling up to the bottom of the hill. Then she looked back at me. "Bye, Indigo."

Chapter
7

An hour later I walked back through the woods to the art studio. The floodlights from outside came in through the windows and fell on the tables and books and brushes and paints, making everything soft and hazy. Making me feel safe, like everything would be okay.

The air-conditioning unit above the door was on, and I stood under it for a minute, enjoying the cool air on my neck and back. Then I flipped on the lights, slipped off my shoes, and walked barefoot across the cool concrete floor to the back, where my self-portrait sat on an easel.

A blue-black blob surrounded by a hell of nothingness.

After a whole month of trying to paint myself—staying late after school, then retreating to my studio until Mom made me come in for dinner; returning to my tiny pine shed until Daddy made me go to bed; sneaking back out again until my forearm and fingers ached so bad I couldn't stand it—that's all I had. Every other attempt had gone in the trash.

My dark skin, big lips, and the small gap between my teeth were always easy. The way my long neck connected to my broad, bony shoulders was no problem. But I could never capture the most important part of myself, what Mr. Marshall called the immaterial essence or soul. And trying felt like hell.

But how was I supposed to paint the innermost part of myself with everything around me changing? With everything inside me pushing and pulling and whirling around? So much felt unknown, impossible to see. And it was like the more I tried, the less I saw. I was starting to feel like a stranger to myself, and it was terrifying.

That's why I'd painted the blue-black blotch over my face. But doing that had only turned me into a faceless stranger. And she was a straight-up beast.

I wanted to take an X-Acto knife from my art bin and slash her into a million pieces. Or throw her over Gigi's fire pit and watch her burn. But I settled on taking her off the easel and sliding her behind a tall wood-framed mirror leaning against the wall.

For a second I felt relieved. Then I looked in the mirror and thought, *I hate you, too.* But something deeper within told me that was a lie. So I thought, *I wish I was someone else.* But again, the truth wouldn't let that wish stick. So I turned my anger toward the pink stars on my jumpsuit and swore to cut every one of them out.

I took off my clothes.

Staring at myself in the mirror in my bra and panties, I wondered why small boobs didn't look as good on me as they looked on Lena. *Was it my height? My prominent collarbones? The massive birthmark above my belly button?*

Scissors. I need scissors, I told myself, furiously trying to get back on track.

I found my art bin and flipped it open. The red envelope from Miles still sat on the top tray. With my friends not asking about it every five seconds, I'd forgotten it was there.

I picked it up and ran its edge along the bottom of my nose, inhaling the faint scent of spearmint gum. I let the smell carry me back to being alone in the studio after school with Miles painting across the room.

From behind my canvas, I snuck a peek at him. At his short, blond afro that blended with his light-brown skin. At his sideburns that trailed off to meet the top of his jaw—bones high and pronounced, always holding his pale pink lips slightly open when he was painting.

He mouthed something to me I couldn't understand.

What? I asked, frowning in confusion.

Please come back, he mouthed again.

And I did.

We spent all summer together painting in my tiny art shed. Every afternoon we shared a bowl of strawberry ice cream to cool down—his lips then my lips, his lips then mine gliding over the same sweet spoon. Then before going back to school in the fall, we dyed our hair complementary colors: blue and orange. Returned as a power painting couple, a Frida Kahlo and Diego Rivera or a Jacob Lawrence and Gwendolyn Knight.

The drum sound of a text message interrupted my fantasy, and I turned to see my phone lit up inside my pants pocket on the floor.

I smiled. *I swear my girls have a sixth sense!* I thought as I bent down to get my phone, preparing to respond with a GIF of a crystal ball. I missed my friends.

Justine: *About to order the pizza. Should I get the norm*

Dani: *I just care about the pepperoni*

Cara: *Cheese for me please*

Justine: *So no veggie*

Dani: *You know Ebony was the only one who ate that mess*

Justine: *Okay so I'll get two mediums. One pepperoni and one cheese*

Dani: *Cool*

Cara: *Sounds good*

I'd dreamed of my friends being so devastated after I left that they couldn't bear having another slumber party without me. I knew that wasn't happening. But I'd at least hoped they'd eat a slice of veggie pizza in my name.

Y'all do realize I'm still on this group chat, right, I typed then quickly deleted. I wasn't about to give them any more reasons to feel sorry for me.

In their minds, there were a million. Sorry I couldn't get Chick-fil-A or Starbucks all the time. Sorry because I had to downgrade to the free version of Spotify. Sorry I couldn't buy at least one cute thing when we went to the mall. Not even eyeliner or gloss. Sorry I had to check books out of the library instead of ordering them online. Sorry for the cold grilled cheese sandwich I brought for lunch every day instead of buying something from the taco or pizza bars.

Trying to sound unbothered, I finally texted: *Pour out a little Sprite for your girl*

Justine: *You know it*

Dani: *My bad Ebony! Didn't realize you were in this chat. Veggie pizza still sucks though lol*

It made sense that they would start another group chat without me, but learning about it still hurt. To cover it up, I texted, *Actually I changed my name back to Indigo. It totally makes sense with my life here.* Like I had it all together. Like I was spending my days happily painting, hanging with new friends, and swimming in the lake. Totally fine with my old life getting further and further away from me.

Cara: *That's awesome. I've missed calling you Indigo. It fits you so well*

I desperately wanted to ask, *How so?* But I wrote back: *It really does.* Clearly I didn't know what I was talking about. I could never go back to being who I was and had no idea who I was becoming. I couldn't even paint myself, and painting was *my* thing. The weight of it all plus my friends moving on without me was too much. Tears started to flow, and I lay down on the cold concrete next to my jumpsuit.

Dani: *That's dope Indigo*

My phone rang. It was Justine, trying to start a four-way

FaceTime. She was my closest friend in the group, the one I'd met the summer after sixth grade at an art camp. She always called immediately if I ever texted anything remotely important. *Texting is not the place to discuss big things,* she always said. *Meaningful things have to be spoken about.*

But I didn't pick up because I knew she'd hear the sadness in my voice. Plus, I was in my underwear.

Me: *It's too loud to talk where I am. Talk tomorrow*

Dani: *Dang partying on a Monday*

Me: *What's a Monday in summer*

Justine: *Jealous!*

Dani: *Me too!*

Cara: *Me three!*

Their responses felt like a tiny victory. They didn't need me to have fun, and I didn't need them, either. At least as far as they knew.

Have fun at the slumber party! I added, trying to slather the I'm-good impression on extra thick. And after I hearted a slew of *Thanks,* I stood up, found some scissors in the bottom of my art bin, and spent the next two hours cutting the stars out of my jumpsuit.

What
She
Missed

The large tube of acrylic paint that hung upside down from a binder clip on the back wall with *Indigo Black* printed on its label. Two years before she'd picked it out of a sale bin because she liked the name. But soon after she'd forgotten she had it. And soon after that, forgotten ever picking it up.

She didn't even remember when she changed her name to Indigo. Or back to Ebony.

She didn't even pay attention to the name when she grabbed it out of a box her dad had packed full of all the random paints he'd found in her drawers. Or when she quickly screwed off the top, squeezed the black paint onto a round-tipped brush, and painted an oval over her face.

Her dad had brought the box of paints to Alula Lake and clipped Indigo Black up between Chromatic Black and Evergreen Black in her new studio. But she hadn't noticed yet.

Chapter 8

*F*or over a week, I avoided the studio. It was easy to ignore while racing Jalen down to the lake every morning. Not as easy when Jalen had to go to his second job at Stevie's and I was stuck in the house with Mom doing Zumba in the living room. Really not easy when I had to walk directly past the studio to meet Jalen on the back of his pickup truck every night. And on the way home—having just stared into the sky's wide eyes and listened to the cicadas and debated Jalen about books and movies and music and the root of all evil (Jalen always argued money; I insisted power)—it felt impossible.

Some nights I'd walk up to the studio window, look through the light-soaked darkness, and stare at my self-portrait peeping out at me from behind the mirror. But I never went inside.

Until the evening of Juneteenth.

Jalen, his dad, and his dad's girlfriend had been over all day for a cookout to celebrate. At sunset, when the mosquitoes started biting, everybody went inside. Then the adults put on Mary J. Blige and started playing spades. Jalen and I didn't know anything about spades, so we decided to go back outside, start a fire, and roast some marshmallows. The smoke would keep the annoying little bloodsuckers away.

"Yo! When am I going to get a new portrait?" Jalen shouted.

Picking up a dead juniper branch along the edge of the trees, I turned and saw him walking toward the studio. I wanted to yell, *Hold up a second! This was not part of the plan!* But it was too late. I hurried back and dropped the dry wood I'd been gathering into the fire pit before following Jalen inside.

Waning sunlight was still spilling in through the windows, and it occurred to me that I hadn't seen this space in this light, when day was turning into night. I looked at my art hanging on the walls and sitting on tables with cautious hope, like it might show me something new about myself.

"Dang, it's hot in here," I said, and grabbed the remote control to the air-conditioning unit off the pedestal by the door. The pedestal was made of carved ebony with a girl as one of its four legs. Her chin and fingers gripped the edge of the small table, like she was trying to pull herself up.

Jalen didn't seem to mind the heat. He was staring at a painting of my bedroom from third grade. I walked up and stood behind him. My Care Bears comforter was on point, but my linear perspective was not. Everything looked flat except the bed, which was lopsided. Still, it felt like home.

On the same wall, a charcoal close-up of my fifteen-year-old smile. Jalen stepped closer to it, I thought to examine how realistically I'd rendered all the cracks in my lips. But then he ran his pointer finger down the gap between my two front teeth, almost touching the paper but not. I'd done that plenty of times, moved by the same impetus that made me trace my gap with the tip of my tongue. But his teeth were perfect, so I wondered what moved him.

"Was this your house in Houston?" he asked, walking up to a painting of the tire swing that hung from the huge live oak tree in our front yard. As a kid, I'd swung on it for hours, intermittently standing on the tire, climbing the rope, and slapping the strong arm of the tree before climbing back down.

"Yeah," I answered, looking at the house in the background, starting to cool down. I stared at its terra-cotta brick and black door. Imaged sliding my silver key into its lock after a long day at school, dropping my backpack on the bench in the foyer, and heading to the kitchen to make myself a grilled cheese sandwich. Then a girl with short, jagged bangs waltzed in, sat down at the counter, ate my sandwich, and headed to my old room. I walked out of the house and away from the painting, wishing I would've snatched my sandwich out of that girl's mouth, imaginary or not.

Jalen continued making his way around the studio, studying my paintings. A clump of light-blue toothpaste caked on my bathroom sink. A lucky dollar bill I'd found crumpled up outside the corner store. Mom's slingback pumps leaning on Daddy's Timberlands at the front door. Chick-fil-A waffle fries spilling out on a napkin. A leaf cluster from the cemetery the day we buried Glamma Ella. My strawberry lip gloss sitting pretty on my dresser.

I felt so exposed, like Jalen was inside me, cruising through all my memories and the random things I'd found interesting. But it was weirdly comfortable. I liked him seeing parts of me he'd never seen before.

Until his eyes wandered too far.

"What's this?" he asked, reaching for the self-portrait I'd hidden behind the mirror.

"Nothing," I said, racing over to push it farther into hiding.

"Wait, wait. What are you doing?"

"Um, isn't it obvious?"

"But your work is dope. The level of detail. The subjects you choose. So simple, but they say so much. This stuff is way more advanced than what you were painting before."

"You mean when I was in elementary school?"

"Okay, I admit that came out stupid. But I guess what I'm trying to say is that seeing all of this reminds me of how much I've missed. Of you . . . of your art . . . your life. And now that I've gotten to see a little bit, I want to see it all."

His expression was so sincere that I thought about dragging my self-portrait out and telling him about my problems with everything changing and losing hope and wanting to cry every time I thought about getting in the lake and not being able to see myself clearly. But the idea of divulging so much made my head hurt.

I walked away from the painting and leaned against Gigi's old wooden table. "You can see everything else," I finally replied, "just not that."

"Why? What's up with that one?"

"It's just . . . it's not finished, okay," I said, my tone going high and loud in a way I usually reserved for Mom. I lowered my eyes.

"It's cool, it's cool," he responded in a soft voice. And then, "Wait, is that the one you still haven't turned in."

"Yeah," I answered, looking down at the chipped purple polish on my toes.

"That dickhead Mr. Marshall."

I laughed and looked up, impressed that he remembered.

"Okay, forget all that. Back to my original question. When am I going to get a new portrait?" he asked, sitting down on the stool beside the empty easel.

"Dang, the sunset is crazy," I said. Behind him, the sky had darkened to a soft pink glow.

He turned around, starred at it for a few seconds, and replied, "If that's not the perfect backdrop, then I don't know what is. We need to get started."

"Hold up. You want me to paint you right now?"

"Yeah, the sky ain't waitin' on nobody."

I'd probably painted Jalen over a hundred times, but that evening I didn't even have the confidence to try. Panicked, I lied. "I don't really work like that anymore. These days, so much detail goes into my portraits that I like to paint them from photographs."

"It doesn't have to be perfect. You can do one of those quick studies you always used to do. Like that one right there," he said, pointing behind me.

I turned and saw a painting of Justine propped up against a mason jar on the table. I'd painted it the first day of art camp as we waited for our dads to pick us up. She was sitting cross-legged in the grass, holding a roll of crackers, with crumbs on her smiling lips. She'd kept the painting all these years and given it back to me the morning I left Houston with a note that said, *From day one.* I didn't want to think about it. "Weren't we were supposed to be roasting marshmallows?"

"All right, all right. But can you at least take my picture? That way you can be working on it."

"You just won't quit, will you," I said, sliding my phone out of the back pocket of my jean shorts.

Jalen threw his hat on the floor and sat up straight on the stool.

I stared at his strong silhouette against the dark pink glow of the sky and bent down to capture it at a good angle. "Good, now turn to the side."

He did.

I took the photo and it clicked. "Okay, yeah. Now stand up."

He pushed the stool out of the way, stood sideways with his hands in the pockets of his jogging shorts, and looked straight ahead.

"Do it, then," I said, admiring his confidence. *Click.*

Then he turned toward me and gazed directly at the camera. This was easy for him.

Click.

He tilted his head down slightly to the right, then to the left, subtly flowing from one position to the next without me asking.

Click. Click. Click.

This was not the same Jalen I'd left when I was ten. I'd missed a lot of him, too. "Dang, dude. You didn't tell me you were a model."

He laughed with his whole chest, and it was so beautiful I rushed at him to capture it up close.

Click.

Chapter 9

A few days later, we drove to town, which was just over the hill, halfway between the north and south ends of the lake. Left elbow hanging out of his window, Jalen waved hello to a lady in white spandex as we passed the dollar store on Main Street. Gave a head nod to an old man in red basketball shorts with a cigarette hanging from his mouth walking out of Catfish King. Shouted, "Celooo," to a young dude with music blasting from his backpack riding his bike along the side of the road.

On McCabe Boulevard we passed Grace Redeemer Baptist Church. It had a big banner tied between two red oaks that read "155th Annual Homecoming, August 2nd." Seeing the banner reminded me of the installations Gigi did for homecoming every summer. Of Daddy driving up. Of smoking pits and paper plates heavy with meat. Of playing tag with Jalen and other kids while the grown-ups slammed down dominoes.

Homecoming, I said to myself, as if remembering an old friend.

"I have to make a quick stop. Stevie needs me to pick up some things," Jalen said before turning onto Isiah Byrd Boulevard, the street that ran straight up a hill before winding back and forth down to the lake on the other side. At the summit, he pulled up to a warehouse with a huge Art Nouveau squid painted on the front above the words "Deep Blue Hardware and Parts" and put the truck in park.

I didn't remember the warehouse, but I did remember the view of the lake off to the east. Gigi used to drive up here to an herbal shop a little farther down the hill. I quickly stepped out of the truck and walked to the edge of the parking lot.

Below, there was a massive stretch of sparkling blue surrounded by tree-covered hills. Standing high above the lake in the haze of the sun, memories filled me—sweet memories that seemed to be trying to tell me something.

Bells chimed behind me, and I looked back. Jalen was

holding the glass door to the warehouse open for me, and I could see that he wanted to keep things moving. I turned away from the lake and the memories, wishing I'd heard what they were trying to say.

Inside, a high wood-beamed ceiling floated over rows and rows of neatly organized wooden shelves. On all four walls, above the displays, large photographs of the lake hung in black frames. I walked toward one that had captured a golden mist over the still blue water at sunrise.

"Ebony," Jalen called. He was standing at the front of the store with a girl who was behind the counter. Busy looking at the photographs, I hadn't even noticed her.

Her hair was slicked back with a middle part that perfectly complemented the swoops and swirls she made with her edges. She wore an acid-washed jumpsuit and a multicolored bandana tied around her neck in a double knot that seemed to scream, *I'm not like you. I know how to take fashion risks and land them.*

I immediately decided that I didn't like her. That she had some kind of nerve.

I walked up to the counter, wishing I'd kept on my rose appliqué headband. I'd put it on and taken it off and put it on and taken it off and ended up with it off because I was worried about it being too much. "Hi, I'm Indigo," I said, hoping she couldn't tell that I thought her outfit was cuter than mine.

"Oh, my bad. That's right," said Jalen.

"Hey," she said, "love your name. I'm Genesis."

I loved her name, too, but just said, "Thanks."

"Y'all don't remember each other?" Jalen asked.

We both shook our heads no.

"Not even a little bit? Maybe from Homecoming?"

Again, it was a . . . no.

"Well, y'all should link up being that y'all are both artists. Indigo is an amazing painter. And as you can see, Genesis got skills with the camera," Jalen said, looking around at the photographs on the walls.

"Wait, you took these pictures of the lake?" I blurted out with a level of excitement I immediately regretted.

"Yeah, it was awhile back. I mostly do portraits now, but I still like to shoot landscapes. Especially living out here. What do you like to paint?"

Nothing anymore, I said to myself, and then aloud, "Anything, really. I like to switch things up."

"That's cool."

I spotted a book cover lying on the counter, with three

bare-chested dudes wearing black pants in a lush field. A thick green ribbon hung from the book's spine that said, "I Can Make You Feel Good." I'd never seen the book before and wanted to know if its pages lived up to its promise. But when I looked back up at Genesis, she had this eager look on her face, like she couldn't wait for me to ask about the book. So I didn't.

She gave me a smile that said, *Maybe next time.*

Her sincerity made me uncomfortable, and I glanced away.

"So whatcha got for me?" Jalen asked and leaned forward on his elbows, the drawstring of his blue bucket hat grazing the counter.

"Let me see." Genesis looked at some items on a steel utility cart beside the register. "A spare prop, coil, distributor cap and rotor, water pump, and some hose clamps. Need anything else?"

"Oh, we're out of zip ties, too."

"Aisle twelve, section F, toward the bottom."

"Bet," Jalen said, and walked off.

I didn't want to be left alone with Genesis. She made me feel insecure, but not in the same way Lena had. Lena was such a departure from me that she was easy to admire.

Plus, she was older and always had troubles of her own. But Genesis looked my age and seemed perfect—creative, genuine, responsible, and totally secure in herself. Torture to be around.

She started ringing up the items on the cart.

"So, you work here in the summers?" I asked, uncomfortable with the silence.

"Yeah."

I felt a tinge of guilt about the fact that I'd never thought about getting a summer job, even with everything my family was going through. "You like it?"

"It's not bad. It's my dad's store. He just opened another one in Nolula, so I'm helping out."

"Nolula?"

"Yeah, it's what they're calling the north side of Alula Lake these days."

I laughed under my breath. "So, I guess white people are moving in?"

"Well, rich people. But yeah, a decent number of them are white. Folks have been moving in for years now. And building big, expensive houses with private boat slips and things. I don't know what it's going to do to our town. I mean, do they care about our history? Do they care about us being a freedom colony? I doubt it. But I can't lie, they've been great for business."

I thought about the stories Gigi used to tell me. About how Alula Lake was started in the late nineteenth century by two brothers and a sister who had previously been enslaved. How they'd been brave enough to go out into the wilderness to find land for their people despite the possibility of being killed by the KKK. And they weren't the only ones. Hundreds of independent black communities sprang up in Texas during the Jim Crow era after the Civil War, as people sought free places to live. Places white folks had abandoned or didn't want to be. Like Alula Lake, which used to flood until about sixty years ago when a group decided to build a dam upstream along the Guadalupe River to create a lake of their own.

Part of me wanted to share the things Gigi had taught me. Maybe even suggest we hang out sometimes. But a different part—small, jealous, and stubborn—thought I'd already said too much to the girl I didn't like. I turned away from her and started walking toward the door. "Dang, Jalen! Would you come on!"

"I'm coming! I'm coming!" Jalen said, half jogging toward the counter.

When I turned back, something about Genesis looked slighted deflated.

I wanted to be happy about it, but I felt like a dick.

When Jalen gave her the zip ties, Genesis immediately filled up with squeaky laughter. He must've said something funny, but I didn't hear it.

Whatever it was turned even funnier and then hilarious, her and Jalen cracking up.

Still standing by the door, I watched them. Bitter I wasn't in on the joke. Bothered by the closeness I smelled in the air.

To cover it up, I took the strawberry-flavored gloss from my cross-body pouch, applied a thick coat to my lips, and pretended not to care.

Chapter
10

"I'm not getting on that sailboat," I told Jalen as we took a right into the parking lot. A large blue-and-beige sign with an anchor in the center read "Stevie's Boat and Slip Rental."

"I know. You already said that."

"I'm serious, Jalen. Don't think you're gonna get me out there and I'm gonna change my mind. Because I'm not."

"I just want to show it to you. That's all," he said and turned off the engine.

He grabbed the big box of stuff he'd bought from the back of the truck and we walked toward a double-wide trailer, gravel crunching beneath my good pair of black Converse. Behind the trailer there were two long wooden docks, lined with boats stretching out into the water. I eyed them, trying to guess which one Jalen was saving his money for.

A screen door slammed. "Is that Ebony Jones?" A small woman walked down the steps of the trailer, smacking on gum.

I smiled politely, trying to remember her. But I couldn't.

Jalen started to correct her about my name. "She actually goes by—"

I hit him in the arm.

"What?" Jalen said under his breath.

She was wearing a Prince T-shirt, cutoff jean shorts, and small braids up in a high ponytail. Looked like a teenager until you got close enough to see her wrinkles and freckles.

I ignored Jalen and shyly walked into the woman's hug.

She squeezed me and then pulled away, but still held on to my forearms. "Looking just like Butchie," she said with minty-smelling breath.

Butchie was the name people in Alula Lake called Daddy. I hadn't heard it in forever and it made me smile.

She gave my arms a good squeeze and let them go. "Glad to have you back, baby."

"Thanks."

"Sorry to run out on y'all," she said, starting to walk off backward. "But me and the mister have a hot date tonight.

They've got *Waiting to Exhale* playing down at the drive-in. Feel free to sail *Honeypie*, though. Just be sure to lock up everything when y'all are out."

"Yes, ma'am," Jalen replied.

She turned and walked off toward an old Bronco, the only other vehicle in the parking lot.

"Honeypie?" I teased Jalen, walking up the steps to the trailer. I held the door open for him. "You didn't tell me that you made the boat your girlfriend. I'm gonna have to tell Genesis you're cheating on her." My last sentence surprised me. *What do I care if he's dating Genesis?* I told myself. But clearly, I wanted to know.

"First of all, Genesis and I aren't like that," he said, shifting the box in his arms to get through the doorway. "And secondly, that boat has been *Honeypie* since my mom—"

The way he stopped midsentence made me want to wrap my arms around him. When I used to come to Alula over the summers, his mom waited tables during the day and sang the blues at Big Baby Red's at night. But a few years ago, Daddy told me she'd decided to try her luck in New York. And last year Daddy mentioned that she hadn't been back since. I wanted to ask Jalen when he'd last talked to her, but joined him in pretending he hadn't mentioned her. "Oh my gosh. It's freezing in here," I said once I got inside the trailer.

"It'll warm up. Stevie always turns off the air when she leaves. But we won't be in here long anyway," he said, walking past a round rack of life vests.

"Did she have this place when I was here?" I asked, eyeing a rack of T-shirts.

He set the bags on the counter behind a stand with sunscreen, mosquito spray, and chips. "Yeah. You don't remember?"

"I mean, it *has* been six years. And anyhow, I don't think Gigi ever brought me here. You know she didn't really mess with boats like that," I said, holding up a cropped tee with "Alula Lake" in airbrushed graffiti letters on the front.

From behind the counter, he pointed a remote above my head and turned off the TV hanging in the far corner of the room playing *Survivor*. "So, you're telling me you don't remember that time Stevie rescued us?"

"Um, no."

"When we swam out to the lighthouse right before that flash flood and all the land around it went underwater, and she came to save us on her boat?"

"Save us? Boy, what are you talking about?" I put the shirt back and tried to remember. But all my memories of us swimming to the lighthouse blurred together.

He gave me an exasperated look and opened a cabinet full of keys hanging by white numbered circles. He lifted number eight from a hook, the only one with a worn brass compass attached. "You seriously don't remember that time we swam out to the lighthouse, and it started to pour down?"

An image of heavy rain falling outside a window flashed across my mind.

"The ground level got covered in water within the first ten minutes we were there," he said. He slid the key into the pocket of his navy swim trunks and started rummaging through a drawer. "It would've been *way* too hard to swim all the back in that weather. If Mama G wouldn't have sent Stevie to come get us, I don't know what would've happened."

"You're so dramatic," I said, starting to remember. How we sat on the second level of the old, abandoned lighthouse playing rock, paper, scissors. How the waves below and the rain outside mixed with our voices and bounced all around us. "We probably would've just sat there playing like we'd been doing."

"But it was getting dark," he said, heading toward the back door.

I followed. "Oh, yeah, and we lit those candles that are

always up there. It was magical," I said, remembering how the candlelight danced on the curved walls.

"We were in danger, Eb—Indigo!" he exclaimed, and opened the door for me.

I laughed, stepped out, and said, "Always the worrywart."

He shook his head and started walking toward the dock on the right. "Nah, always the one paying attention."

A dragonfly skimmed the surface of the lake below me and flew off toward the setting sun. As I walked along the dock, I imagined Stevie's life. Being out on the lake every day with its bugs and birds and heat and then going back into the trailer to cool down and do paperwork while watching reality TV. Simple but she seemed happy. A lot happier than Mom ever was going downtown every day in a suit.

"I literally cried tears of joy when I heard Stevie's motorboat pull up." Jalen still wasn't finished trying to relay the gravity of the lighthouse situation.

"Did you really?"

He turned back to look at me. "Yeah, I was scared for our lives!"

I couldn't believe I'd remembered the night so differently. I thought about how the ride back was even more fun. Stevie gave us a tarp to cover our heads and Jalen and I each held onto one end. And when the wind got underneath the tarp, it felt like a cape. It felt like we were flying.

Jalen turned around and waved his right arm in the direction of a sailboat with a glossy, amber-colored wooden exterior. "This is *Honeypie*."

"Ooh, pretty."

He stepped onto the boat. "Come on, let me show you around," he said, holding his hand out for me.

But I was still operating in the if-he-can-do-it-I-can-do-it mode from childhood. I took a large step from the dock down into the boat without taking his hand and lost my balance.

Jalen caught me by the arms and steadied me. "You good?"

"I'm fine," I said, taking back my weight. "The boat is just wobbly."

He laughed. "Yeah, being on the water will do that."

"Shut up," I replied, smiling. "Are you going to give me the grand tour or what?"

For the next ten minutes, he walked around the boat talking about the mainsail, boom, mast, centerboard, and a whole bunch of other things I can't remember. It didn't get interesting until he got to the cockpit.

I picked up the black walkie-talkie–looking part of the radio, brought it to my mouth, and said, "Mayday, Mayday."

"*M'aider*," he said in a French accent.

"What?"

"Help me," he said. "That's what Mayday means. It's from the French expression *Venez m'aider*, which translates as 'come and help me.'"

"*Venez m'aider*," I tried to repeat but it got jumbled coming out of my mouth. "I forgot you take French."

"Yep, and Spanish. Figure I'll need as many languages as I can get. Anyway, the cabin is down here," he said and stepped into the enclosed part of the boat.

I slid the walkie-talkie back into its holder and followed.

"Take your time. It's steep."

He wasn't lying. I held on to the wood railing to make sure I didn't fall as I went under. "It's like a tiny house in here," I said when I got down.

"Yep, that's exactly what it's meant to be."

A bench with burnt-orange cushions extended along one side of the boat and into the back corner, where it widened out. I slid by Jalen and went to lie down on it.

"Pretty comfy, huh?"

"Yeah," I said and imagined myself waking up after a

good night's sleep and opening the super-short curtains to a bright sun and blue sea. I imagined grabbing a book from the wooden shelf behind the bench. Fixing something to eat on the ministove and washing dishes in the minisink. "This is sick," I said and sat up.

"Thanks. Stevie said she'd sell it to me for seven grand. I've already saved up forty-three hundred, so I should definitely have the rest by the time we graduate."

We, I thought, resisting the urge to get mad about not graduating from Houston's Academy of the Arts. "I'm so proud of you, Jalen! You're making it happen!"

"Gots to!" he replied.

Earlier that week on the back of the truck, Jalen had told me that he didn't plan on going to a four-year college. After graduation, he wanted to sail *Honeypie* to South Carolina, where he'd start a sailing tour business and take some marine engineering and language classes at the community college. He'd stay in South Carolina until he was able to level up to a new boat. Then he'd move to Florida, where he'd do the same thing. Then to Mexico.

Looking at Jalen standing in the minikitchen of his future boat, I remembered how I'd always doubted him growing up. Sailing the world had sounded like such a big dream that

I assumed he'd give it up and switch to something more normal. It was awful, but I thought I'd be the one making my
dreams come true, not him.

"Well, that's about it. Not much more to see."

"Thanks for my tour. You and *Honeypie* are cute together,"
I said, managing to smile.

"Whatever," he replied, laughing.

Up on deck, the sun was a little lower in the sky and the
faint smell of firewood was in the air. I took a deep breath in,
closed my eyes, and let the smell mingle with memories of
Gigi stirring her canvases in the large vat above the fire pit.

Jalen looked at me. "Yeah, they get the bonfires started
early at The Cove," he said.

"Oh, another party?"

"I don't think they ever stop. But from what I overhear
from Lena, things tend to crank up when the sun goes down."

I grabbed one of the wooden handles on the steering
wheel and gave it spin. "You feel like sailing by there?"

"Oh, so *now* you wanna go sailing?"

I spun the wheel again. "I just want to see what's going
on. We don't have to stay long."

Jalen grabbed a handle and stopped the spinning. "Sorry,
it's not my scene."

"Have you even been?"

"Trust, I don't need to. This is not the first time some rich kid here for the summer has thrown a party."

I grabbed the wooden handle beside the one he was holding. "But *I* need to. I've never been to a party here. And I don't know anyone else."

"Well, I told you that my boys Adrick and Quentin are gone for the summer, but I can get Genesis and some other people from school together. Ooh, we can float the river tomorrow! That's always fun."

"You know I'm not getting in that water."

"Why not?"

"Same reason I'm not getting in the lake. I don't swim anymore."

"But you used to love to swim. Mama G would've wanted you to keep swimming."

I thought about how a fisherman had found her dead, floating in her white swim cap alongside the pier at Cranes Park. She never swam that far, but the wind must've pushed her. I'd wondered what had happened a thousand times. *Had she gotten a cramp? Accidentally taken water in through her nose and choked? How could something she did every day for so many years kill her? Why had God let her die when I still needed her love?*

These were the questions I'd buried for a long time. Then, without warning, they were everywhere inside me again. I couldn't deal. "Forget about it. It's not happening," I finally said.

"Well, we can do something else then."

"Come on, Jalen," I said and tried to push the steering wheel toward him.

"Come on, Indigo," he said, pushing it back.

Then I gave him the same face I used on Daddy when I really wanted something. It was an expression of intense softening that said, *But I'm helpless without you.*

He stared at me for a few tender seconds and then looked down without saying anything.

I took a twisted pleasure in my victory and pressed on. "Plus, I never get to see Lena."

He shot his eyes back up to mine. "You don't need to be hanging with Lena anyway."

I wanted to kick myself for speaking too soon and breaking the spell. "It's not about Lena. I just want to do something other than go down to the lake every day. It's getting boring. I need something else to take my mind off everything. *Please.*"

He let out a big sigh. "Fine, but we're not staying long."

I didn't care how long we stayed. All that mattered was that we were going. I threw my arms around his neck. "Thank you! Thank you! Thank you!"

"Yeah, yeah," he said, backing away and pulling on a rope attached to a silver railing along the edge of the boat.

"Okay, what do you need me to do? I can help sail. But I really don't want to get dunked. I'm too cute for that," I said and did a twirl in my yellow baby-doll dress.

"It's all good," he said, still messing with the rope. "I don't want to take *Honeypie* out this late anyway. Haven't prepped her for a night sail. We can take one of the sport boats."

What
She
Missed

He was helpless without her, too.

Until she started talking again and gave herself away.

He prepared to guard himself forever, keep his eyes wide open for her tricks.

Then she hugged him, and it made him shudder.

No, he told himself. *Eb-Indigo is my friend.*

But a different feeling had already crept in.

The feeling frightened him. Confused him. He pulled away, trying to erase it. Telling himself that her trick had just gotten tangled up with the glow of the sunset. That he needed to straighten it out. Forget about it.

But he'd replay her twirl the rest of the night.

Chapter 11

*G*azing out at the lake from the rocky shoreline was one thing, but to be on top of it—to have its depths beneath me, its blue body all around me, and its spray on my face—was another. Feeling angry or sad or afraid on the boat felt impossible.

I looked over at Jalan, sitting on my right with his flapping bucket hat cinched all the way up to his chin, one hand on the steering wheel and the other on the throttle.

"Faster!" I shouted.

But he didn't push the black lever forward.

"This is amazing!" I yelled anyway.

He gave me a small, closed-lip smile and turned back to the water. He'd been in a mood since he'd agreed to take me to the party.

Too happy to be bothered, I went quiet and tried to memorize the scene at that moment. The two black ravens flying above the massive lake. The darkening sky beyond them. The woody hills below the sky. And the tired orange sun about to lay it down for the night.

We rode like that for fifteen minutes, in our own worlds, in a straight line heading north. Jalen didn't slow down to remind me which inlet led to the Guadalupe River, or the name of the horse ranch along the east shore, or where his grandpa had discovered dinosaur footprints after the megaflood of 1966 uncovered a limestone gorge never seen before. And I didn't ask.

We kept to ourselves until huge houses began poking their faces out from the tree-covered hills. One long and severe with white stucco. Another stony and pointy with shutters. Two with tall, stately columns. A few with arches and clay roofs. Most with pools overlooking the lake, and a boat and a Jet Ski or two.

Jalen slowed down.

"This must be Nolula," I said, looking into the lit windows, trying to spy someone home.

"Yeah, if you want to call it that. But it'll always be the North Side to me."

I got the sense that I was supposed to feel some sort of loss, but I couldn't. The smell of firewood was even thicker here, and I took a deep breath in, consumed with anticipation. "Nolula . . . the North Side, it's all whatever to me!"

Jalen shot me a disgusted look.

I thought about apologizing. Explaining that my excitement had made my words come out wrong. But instead, I said. "Don't be mad."

"Mad?"

"Yeah, about taking me to the party," I replied, trying to change the subject.

"I could miss it, but I'm not mad," he said, driving by a red-and-white sign that said, "No Wake Zone." He pulled the lever back to slow all the way down.

"It's summer. Don't you want to let loose?"

"Not like this."

"I swear you're such an old man," I said, laughing.

"If not wanting to get drunk and act stupid for no reason makes me an old man, then I'll be that," he said and loosened the drawstring on his hat.

"Who said anything about getting drunk?"

"You've obviously never been to a lake party."

We went quiet again, the darkening trees wrapping

around us. Then a few minutes later, I spotted a fire. Using my phone as a mirror, I cleaned up my cobalt blue eyeliner, fixed my windblown bun, and reapplied my gloss.

"I still can't believe they sold this place," Jalen said.

I took one last look and told myself, *You cute.* "Wait, which part of it was theirs?" I asked, gazing at the cabins dotted along the shore and resting in the hills.

"All of it. Over a hundred acres."

"Dang!"

"I know. It's been in their family for six generations. You see that small stone cabin over there?" Jalen asked, pointing to the house at the end of the bay.

"I think so."

"Well, it's over a hundred fifty years old."

"Seriously?"

"Yeah, obviously it's been updated a lot over the years to make it better for guests. And the floors had to be replaced a few times after floods, but its stones are the original ones."

"How do you know all of this?"

"I did a history report on it for school. I won't put you to sleep you with *all* the details, but the property started out as a family compound and farm. You know, back in the day-day when people were having, like, fifteen kids and each of them were having fifteen more. But then fifty years ago, they opened it up to the public for short-term stays and named it The Cove. It was the only lodging in Alula Lake for decades. But no telling what these new people have planned for it."

Ahead, a boy about our age in some flamingo swim trunks and white Gucci slides walked down the dock and started directing us with big arm motions.

"Ugh, not this dude again," Jalen said.

The boy *was* being extra. All he needed was a neon vest and some orange wands like the people who helped park the planes at the airport. "Who is he?"

"You know, the dude Lena was talking about from Austin or somewhere. He came into Stevie's the other day to rent a boat and got mad when she wouldn't let him take one without a parent or any kind of boater's license. I mean, you should've heard the way he was talking to her. It was like he had never heard the word 'no' before. Boy didn't have no home training."

"Who does he think he is," I said, eyeing the way his strong chest and biceps flexed as he waved his arms. The way his short sandy locs hung down in his sun-kissed face. *A surfer or a football player?* I wondered. Either way, I liked what I saw.

Jalen angled the boat toward the corner of the slip.

"Turn the wheel! Turn the wheel!" the surfer-football boy shouted, moving his arm in a big circle.

"This fool," Jalen mumbled. "Turn the wheel? I got it, anyway, but what kind of direction is that?"

"So stupid," I agreed, and laughed, keeping the smile on my face a few seconds past natural in case the boy was looking.

Jalen reversed, lined the boat up a bit more, pulled in slow, and turned the engine off.

The boy strolled over to the left side of the boat and held out his hand for me.

I took it and his eyes moved over my legs as he helped me up onto the dock. Unlike my boobs, I knew my legs were good. Strong for no reason, like I ran track or something. And I was happy that they had the boy's attention.

We exchanged names and hellos, unembarrassed to hold each other's eyes, and I imagined him kissing me and telling me he's never felt like this before. But I was stiff, unsure of how to move my mouth and lips. Then he was Miles, saying, *See, that's exactly why I didn't bother*. My fantasy had quickly turned all the way left and I shook my head trying to escape it.

"Is something wrong?" Craig asked.

"Long story," I answered, hoping to sound more mysterious than weird.

"Maybe later?"

"Yeah."

Then he hopped down into the boat and pulled Jalen in for a handshake-hug-dap, finished off with a snap, like they'd been tight their whole lives. "Bro, let me take this out for a quick spin," he said, sliding past Jalen to get behind the wheel.

"Nah, it's not my boat," Jalen replied.

Craig turned on the ignition anyway.

"Whoa, whoa, whoa," Jalen said, reaching over him. "Take it easy, homie." He turned the engine off again, slid the key out of the ignition, and slipped it into his pocket.

"I know how to drive a boat, dude. And I'm not talking about those little Jet Skis over there," Craig said, pointing to two three-seaters in the slips on the other side of me. "We have a huge boat that I drive all the time on Lake Travis. And it's fast! I'm telling you, I did a hundred in it one time."

"I don't doubt you."

"So, you'll let me drive, then?"

"Sorry, bruh."

"Why? You don't trust me?"

"I literally just met you. And like I said, it's not my boat."

"Come on, Jalen. Stop acting like an old man," I said, already sorry. When I'd called him an old man before, it was a joke between friends. But there was nothing funny about saying it then. I didn't think he should let Craig drive the boat, either. I was just uncomfortable with the tension.

"It's not happening. I don't know what else y'all want me to say."

"No worries, bro," Craig said, and patted Jalen on the shoulder, like he'd won anyway. "Come on. I'm being a bad host. Let me show you around."

Chapter 12

Craig's version of showing us around consisted of pointing toward the people near the fire and rushing off in the opposite direction.

As Jalen and I walked up, I saw Lena sitting on a log, talking to a girl with a bleached-blond buzz cut. They were both wearing chokers and holding red plastic cups.

A football flew over Lena's head, and she looked at a boy with a perfectly round afro making the catch and then at me. I smiled at her, but she ignored me and turned back to her buzz-cut friend.

Her rudeness stung, but I told myself it was admirable. Told myself that girls shouldn't be expected to smile all the time and that I, too, should free myself of the instinct. I recalled the night Mom sent me inside Willie's Grill to pick up our takeout and a man behind the counter with a long gray ponytail and a round belly told me I'd be prettier if I smiled. I wanted to give him the middle finger, but automatically smiled and played it cool. "That's better," he replied. The memory had absolutely nothing to do with Lena ignoring me, but telling myself that it did made me feel better about still wanting to be her friend.

Beside me, a pretty boy with smooth brown skin and a cornrow fade pulled Jalen into a half handshake, half hug.

Pretending to be carefree as I waited to be introduced, I danced to the music blasting from a speaker on a foldout table holding a cooler, a stack of red plastic cups, and bags and bags of chips.

The boy's name was Dom (short for Dominque), and he was Lena's ex-boyfriend turned friend. In fact, the whole party was full of Lena's friends. After Jalen finished talking to Dom, we sat down on the log closest to the lake and took in the scene.

Not as many people as I expected. Lena and the buzz-cut girl, her friend since third grade. Four dudes throwing a football. I thought the two with Jesus pieces were twins, but the gold chain had the silver by a year. Two girls with jumbo box braids in bikinis dancing. And a girl with wavy black hair and bright-red lips off to the side taking selfies.

Ahead, up in the hills, a yellow rectangle popped on, and I spotted Craig talking to someone in the doorway of a cabin. Their silhouettes were beautiful, and I stared until Jalen caught me and gave me a funny look.

A few minutes later, Craig was down on the beach, squeezing between me and Jalen. He wrapped his arms around our shoulders, and I caught a whiff of his scent—musty with a hint of sweet cologne. I didn't mind it at all.

"Sorry about that. Had to check in with my uncle. But don't worry, he's mad young. Really more like a cousin. Only twenty-three, so he won't be trippin' or anything."

"Cool," I responded.

"Have y'all met everybody?" Craig asked

Jalen glanced at him. "Indigo hasn't, but I'll—"

"Hey!" Craig shouted, standing up. He reached into his pocket, grabbed his phone, and cut off the music. "Yo!" he shouted again. "Listen up, everybody, this here is Jalen and Indigo. Jalen and Indigo, this is Meka, Gerri, Sharon, Lena, Rebecca, Dom, Anthony, Eric, Deandre, and Jimmy," he said, pointing to everyone as he went along.

"What up!" yelled Eric, the brother with the gold cross.

"J is in the building!" the big boy named Anthony shouted. I could tell he lifted a lot of weights and ate a lot of food. "You, too, Indigo, my bad!"

I started to smile at him but stopped myself.

"Hey," Meka said beside me, taking a break from posing for her phone.

"Hi," I said back.

Lena didn't even bother to look at me, and it felt like torture. I wanted to be someone she thought was cool or interesting or at the minimum cute. I looked down at my yellow baby-doll dress. I'd seen it on the brown mannequin at the mall a year earlier and it had been love at first sight. But sitting on that log, I found fifty things wrong with it. Beginning with the fact that "baby" was part of its name. Moving on to it being yellow. *Maybe a choker could've balanced it out,* I thought. *At least I'm not wearing that stupid rose headband.*

Craig came back with drinks. "Because you're driving," he said, handing Jalen a bottle of water.

"Thanks, I don't drink anyway," Jalen said.

"Neither do I," Craig responded, and handed me a red cup.

I wanted to say, *Me, either.* Daddy had let me taste his gin once when I was in middle school. But it was nasty, and I hadn't had a sip of alcohol since. Not like I had much oppor-tunity. It was still punch and parents in the next room at the parties I'd been to in Houston. But I took the cup anyway.

"You drink?" Jalen asked me after Craig left.

"No," I said, staring down at the bright-red liquid. Looked like Hawaiian Punch. I brought it up to my nose—not Hawaiian Punch.

"So, why'd you take it then?"

"Relax, I'm not going to drink it," I told Jalen. And I didn't. I balanced it on my crossed legs, until the sky went completely dark and the football game turned into keep-away with Anthony's phone.

"Stop playin'!" he shouted, running past us. His phone flew over our heads, and Eric caught it. Then he threw it over the fire to his brother Jimmy.

"I swear to God if y'all burn up my phone, we gon' fight!"

But the phone kept flying from person to person. And after the two girls with the box braids, Gerri and Sharon, got in on the game, I figured, *What the hell?* I put down my cup (twisting it back and forth into the rocks to make sure it was steady) and stood up. "Over here," I yelled.

Gerri, the one with the polka-dotted bikini, threw me the phone, laughing.

I caught it, laughing too.

Then Lena stood up and reached her hands in the air like she wanted next.

I looked dead at her and threw it to Sharon, trying not to show how worried I was that she'd hate me forever. It could've gone either way, but I figured at least I'd get her attention.

Lena stared at me—hard.

I stared back at her even harder, feeling surprisingly comfortable. I'd been mad at life for months, and no one really understood. But Lena seemed to be right there with me, our eyes held together by our shared anger at the world. It was like she was my middle finger, and I was hers.

Then Lena yelled, "Last one in the lake has to clean up," and everyone took off running toward the water. I couldn't just stand there—I didn't want to be the one stuck cleaning up—so, without thinking, I ran too. As we got closer to the shoreline, people started stripping off their clothes—shorts, T-shirts, bikini tops, swim trunks.

I slowed down and looked back at Jalen. He was still in the same spot on the log by the fire.

I cursed myself, wishing I was sitting beside him. Wishing that I could somehow camouflage my brown skin with the rocks and disappear. Anything but stand there looking too afraid or lame, or whatever else Lena would think, to get naked and get in.

"I see you don't get down like that, either," a voice behind me said. It was Craig, still in his flamingo swim trunks.

I'd never felt more relieved. "Yeah, I don't really swim anymore."

"Why? Because of all your hair?"

"No, my twists are actually good with water. It's the reason my grandmother started doing my hair like this when I was little. I just haven't been swimming in a while, that's all," I said, probably giving him more information than he cared to know.

"Well, I love swimming. But not like this."

"You mean to tell me that you've never been skinny-dipping in Lake Travis?"

"Yeah, plenty of times *by myself*. And once with my ex-girl."

"Oh," I said and imagined our naked limbs gliding through warm water, accidentally touching here and there.

"Anyway, come on. I have something better for us to do," he said. He took my hand and pulled me toward the dock. When we reached the wooden planks, he asked, "You ever been Jet Skiing before?"

"No," I answered, and glanced back at Jalen again.

"Well, you're in for some major fun."

Walking along the dock, still hand in hand with Craig, I twisted my neck to look at Jalen another time. I wanted to tell him that I'd be right back.

"Don't worry, Grandpa will be okay," he said, laughing and pulling a key out of the pocket of his trunks.

I didn't like Craig talking about Jalen like that. "I know *Jalen* will be okay," I said with an attitude. "But he *is* my ride, so I don't want to just disappear on him."

"I won't keep you too long," he responded, seemingly unfazed. Then he stepped down onto the Jet Ski with his left foot, swung his right leg over the long seat, sat down, and scooted up. "Get on."

I looked back at Jalen one last time and mouthed, *Be right back*, hoping the words would reach him telepathically. Then I grabbed Craig's shoulder for balance—strong—and repeated his movements until I was sitting behind him with my inner thighs wrapped around his legs.

Craig started the engine. "All you have to do is hold on tight. That's literally it. Just don't let go."

Chapter
13

*W*e were alone on the lake. I looked out at the black water surrounding us, the black trees, and the black sky with its bright stars and slight moon, and wondered if what I was feeling was what Gigi meant when she used to say, "Nature can give you the peace of God."

I wasn't hungry or thirsty or mad. I wasn't jealous. I didn't want to cry or understand myself. I didn't care about the Incomplete in Art, my future, or being cute. I only felt the wind pressing against my face, the mist of warm water kissing my bare legs, and my whole body squeezing Craig.

"Faster!" I yelled.

The engine roared loader, and wave after wave swelled beneath us, making my butt leave the seat.

"Faster!" I yelled again.

"That's what I'm talking about," Craig shouted over his shoulder.

Another roar and my heart raced with a new surge of energy. The waves came at us even harder, yanking me around. A slip could've sent me flying off. A wrong turn probably could've flipped us. Maybe even killed us. But the wildness coming alive in me didn't care. "Faster," I yelled again and again until it felt like we were flying.

We went somewhere else. A place where I was incapable of telling time. A place that didn't know anything about the world turning. All it knew about was the pleasure of speed and the thrill of risk and the twists and turns and dizzying circles. We went round and round as Craig did these things called doughnuts. Carved our names in the water with sharp turns. Cut through our own wake, jumping over big waves. Water soaked everything up to my neck. Tasted sweet on my lips. Felt warm between my legs.

Not even the moon had a clue what time it was. And neither did the pleasure of Craig's locs tickling my cheeks. Or the deliciousness of holding tight to his strong body while completely letting myself go.

But the old lighthouse knew plenty. It stood tall out on the peninsula at the south end of the lake and had watched everything for a hundred and seventy-five years. As soon as I saw it, I felt it narrowing its black, rectangular window at me, scolding me for being gone way too long.

As we came back into the bay, I talked myself into believing it was possible that Jalen could have been enjoying himself so much that he didn't even notice how long I'd been gone.

But as I started walking down the dock toward the shore, he was already coming toward us.

I started running out of guilt, water gushing out of my sneakers with every step.

When I reached him, all he said was, "You ready?" His voice wasn't harsh, but he didn't look at me and he didn't stop walking toward the boat.

"I'm sorry, Jalen," I said, turning around to follow him. I wanted to give him better words, but I didn't trust myself enough to hide the fact that it was one of the best nights of my life. That even though I felt like a horrible friend, I wouldn't have done anything different.

Craig walked toward us slowly, shoulders light and easy, like he didn't have a single care. "Next time you'll have to drive, Indigo."

I didn't answer, hoping he'd say something to Jalen.

Apologize for keeping me out so late. Invite him to Jet Ski another time. Anything conciliatory. But he didn't.

And Jalen didn't say anything to him, either. Just gave Craig a head nod and kept it moving.

We rode in silence all the way to Ernie's, a convenience store with a fuel dock, not too far from Stevie's on the west shore. When Jalen turned off the engine, I looked over at him, but he kept his eyes straight ahead like he had the whole way there.

I twirled the edge of my wet dress, uncomfortable with how far away he felt. I tried to think of something to say, but nothing was good enough.

"No way I should have Stevie's boat out this late," he finally said, putting the nozzle into the gas tank.

I looked over at him, caught a whiff of gasoline, and briefly enjoyed it. "I know. I'm really sorry."

Eyes still fixed on the nozzle, he said, "I didn't even ask her if I could take this boat out."

I wanted to say "sorry" again, but remembered what Gigi used to say about over-apologizing—one "sorry" was good. Two was plenty. Three was too many—and kept my mouth shut.

After a few moments of silence, Jalen looked over at me. "Two hours, Ebony? Indigo . . . you know what I mean. But two hours? And you didn't even bother to let me know you were leaving. You don't know Craig like that. Nobody does. He could be an even bigger fool than I already think he is. And Jet Skiing can be dangerous. Especially at night. As you can see," he said looking around, "the lake is empty. Mr. Tucker is supposed to be out here patrolling but he's always passed out drunk. It's a joke. If something would've happened to you, there would've been no one to help." His voice was high, and he was speed talking, his frustration pouring out. "What were you thinking?"

I wanted to tell him that he had nothing to worry about. That Craig had skills. That he probably could've driven this boat *easy*, but I knew better. "I wasn't," I said, trying to keep a solemn face as I remembered how free I'd felt.

"I know you were probably just trying to have a little fun," he continued, "but you can't be out here acting like you don't have good sense."

"Good sense?" I replied, face scrunched up, feeling like he'd just called me stupid.

"Yeah, good sense."

"I'm not dumb, Jalen."

"Nobody called you dumb."

"All I'm saying is that if I felt unsafe, I would've made him bring me back."

"Made him?"

"Yeah, made him."

"And what if he didn't feel like coming back? How exactly would you have made him? You were literally on the back of a Jet Ski with some random dude on an empty lake in the middle of the night. Not exactly in a position to make anybody do anything. That's what I mean about having good sense."

I rolled my eyes at the lecture. "Well, Lord knows you have *plenty* of that," I replied, stopping short of adding *Grandpa*.

"As a matter of fact, I do," he popped back like he'd heard the *Grandpa* anyway. "And guess what? My good sense does some *good* things for me. Like keeping me outta trouble and moving me in the ways I'm trying to go. I'd say *good sense* is pretty necessary."

"But so is having fun, Jalen. You should try it sometime."

"I have plenty of fun."

I didn't want to fight Jalen. I wanted to be grateful and sorry, especially after he'd reluctantly taken me to The Cove and I'd ghosted him for hours. I was dead wrong. I needed him to see I understood that. But I didn't know how to back down. "Sure you do," I replied, turning away from him to tend to my wet phone.

Chapter
14

*W*hat I remember most about the next few days was not having any orange juice and Mom doing a lot of Zumba in the living room. Of course, Jalen hadn't come to get me to run down to the lake since the night of the party. And none of my friends from home had texted me, not even by mistake.

Each time I'd gone to the studio, I'd stared at my last blank canvas for hours, afraid of ruining it with a wrong stroke. But I didn't care about any of that, I told myself. My problem was with the orange juice and Mom's Zumba.

On day four of no Jalen, I woke up to the sound of rhythmic drums and horns and immediately started crying. It was almost noon, and I was mad at myself for messing things up with the one person who brought me happiness in Alula Lake. But I convinced myself that I was crying because I hadn't gotten enough sleep.

I wiped my face and stormed out of my room.

Mom was in front of the TV in the living room chest popping in a sports bra and leggings. Way too much for me. I rolled my eyes and hooked a left into the kitchen, hoping someone had finally gone to the store.

I opened the fridge and briefly enjoyed the cool air on my face, neck, and chest before I noticed there was still no juice.

"Seriously?" I yelled, and slammed the refrigerator door.

"What?" Mom called out from the living room.

I walked through the arched doorway between rooms and stood behind her while she shook her hips to some samba music. "Are we so poor that we can't afford orange juice?" I asked, annoyed with how much I sounded like a brat.

"Morning, Indigo," Mom replied. She always ignored my bad attitudes. Probably following the advice of some parenting book she'd read on how to deal with teenage emotions. She had a million books on parenting, which I found infuriating since she'd chosen to outsource most of the job.

It was hard for me to watch her dance, but I sat down on the sofa anyway, envying her boobs and curves and the way she moved her body. So fluid and unselfconscious. It wasn't right for a mother to have a better body than her teenage daughter and be able to move it better than her, too. "We could probably afford some orange juice if you got a real job."

She ignored me and kept dancing, but I could see her fury in the force with which she shook her hips.

"I mean, exactly how long do you plan on dragging this Zumba thing out?" I asked.

She stopped dancing, took a visibly deep breath, and smoothed down the edges of her hair, which weren't cooperating with her bun. She'd stopped making her weekly hair appointments after she lost her job. She tried to maintain her relaxed hair herself, but it needed more help than she could give it. It was rough—puffy at the roots and stringy at the ends. Didn't go with her usual polished look. And neither did the hats she constantly wore to cover it up.

I almost felt sorry for her.

She walked toward me, leaned over to grab the remote on the sofa, pointing her toe (a remnant from her childhood as a ballerina), and paused the three women dancing in unison on the TV.

"You know, Indigo, when I lost my job and couldn't find another one, I had no idea what I was going to do," she said and sat down beside me, wiping the sweat dripping from her face with the strap of her sports bra.

I wondered how she could still smell like a meadow.

"I felt so lost and depressed. But it's funny how some of the worst things in life can hold the biggest opportunities. They're hard to see at first, when things are dark and you think all is lost, but they're there the whole time, waiting to be discovered."

I could sense that she was trying to turn this into a teaching moment, and I wasn't having it. "What in the world are you talking about?"

"All I'm saying is that losing my job ended up being a good thing. For so many years of my life, I thought I needed to make partner. I hinged so much of my worth on my ability to achieve that goal. But I wasn't happy, and I was sacrificing way too much. Most importantly time with you and your father. Being away from home so often was miserable and heartbreaking. But I couldn't see that when I got fired. Or when no one would hire me. It took me awhile—"

"So being broke is wonderful. Having to sell the house and move all the way out here to the middle of nowhere is fantastic."

"I know you can't see it now, but moving out here will be good for us," she said and put her hand on my knee.

"Including you. Have you reached out to that painter I keep telling you about? Mrs. Williams? She teaches at the high school, so you'll see her in the fall, but she said she'd be more than happy to paint with you over the summer. She even offered to help with that incomplete assignment."

"I already finished that," I lied. "And I probably won't see her next year because I don't want to paint anymore."

"What are you talking about? You love painting."

I couldn't tell her how impossible it was to paint myself. How trying made my head hurt and my heart hurt. Made me feel stupid and small. So I went with an easier response, an excuse and weapon all in one. "Forget being broke. I'm not about to be some starving artist putting my so-called passion over my family."

"Is that what you think? But I'll be home way more. I'll get to spend time with you before you go to college. Precious time. I can't get back what we've lost, but I can take advantage of we have left. And I'm serious about Zumba. I start teaching at the gym next week. I know it won't bring in a lot of money right away, but I have a two-year plan to open a dance studio. And your dad has plans to start his own home building company. We're going to be all right, Indigo. Better than all right. You'll see."

I stared straight ahead with all the disgust I could muster. The fact that she would abandon a high-paying career in consulting to teach Zumba pissed me off beyond reason. Maybe because the real things I was mad at her for—always working and leaving for business trips when I was a child, shipping me off every summer, missing almost all of my art exhibitions—I couldn't even approach. I could never admit that I needed her. Wanted her. Felt rejected by her. I could never admit that I was afraid to love her again. I didn't even have the words for it.

My throat began to ache, and I stood up.

She stood up, too, and smoothed back the edges of her hair again. "When your dad gets home with the truck, I'll make sure to pick up some orange juice, okay?"

"Don't worry about it. I can drive to get it myself," I said, looking at her hard. And then I added, "I hope you plan on doing something with that hair of yours before you start teaching. It's a mess."

Her eyes widened in shock, then lowered in hurt.

I'd given my mother plenty of attitude over the years, but I'd never insulted her. A door inside me pushed open and a little girl came running out wanting to throw her arms around her and say, *I'm sorry, Mommy. I love you so much.*

Please forgive me. I'm not myself. But I hadn't hugged Mom in years and wasn't about to start then.

She turned and walked away.

And I stood there, strong will intact, burning with guilt and shame.

What
She
Missed

Pretending to be asleep when her mother came home late from work and opened the door to her room. The bed creaking as her mother crawled in. Not wanting it to end. Her mother's warm body curled behind her. The smell of a meadow. Her hurt melting away. Resting easy, finally.

Chapter 15

"Pinch me," I told Jalen, walking up to him holding out my arm. It was July fourth, and he was sitting in my front yard at the foldout table, which was covered with potato salad, baked beans, coleslaw, grilled corn, watermelon, and potato chips all in plastic-wrapped bowls. Before Jalen, his dad, and his dad's girlfriend arrived, I'd spent all morning and early afternoon helping Mom in the kitchen and then collecting wildflowers for a large centerpiece. It didn't make up for the way I'd behaved a few days earlier, but I was trying.

Jalen acted like I wasn't there and tapped one of the buttonbush buds in the arrangement. Little spiky snowballs.

I sat down beside him and placed my forearm on the table. "Pinch me as hard as you can."

"What?" he finally answered, still staring straight ahead, tapping the white bud.

"I need you to stop being mad at me."

"I'm not mad at you."

"Stop lying. You haven't said two words to me since y'all got here."

"I literally just said five. I'm. Not. Mad. At. You," he said, a tap accentuating each word.

"You're literally giving that flower a whipping."

He looked at me and almost cracked a smile.

"And you haven't come to get me to go to the lake all week."

"I thought the lake was boring."

"See, that's exactly what I'm talking about. Just pinch me so we can get this over with," I said, putting my forearm on top of his. "Hard. Like, really hard."

He moved his arm and mine plopped down beside his. His was darker and redder from all the hours in the sun. Mine was hairier. His was long and smooth with three large veins running diagonally from elbow crease to wrist. I reached for the meatiest part and pinched.

"Ouch!" he whined, and then smiled. "What's wrong with you?"

"I want you to pinch me."

"You know what? I got something better," he said, and started peeling the plastic wrap off the corner of the potato chip bowl.

"Ooh, give me one."

"Don't worry. I'm about to." He grabbed two chips, stacked them, and dumped some hot sauce on top, careful not to splash his fingers.

"You know I love me some hot sauce."

"Oh, I'm not done yet," he said, standing up. He reached for the plate of garnishes (sliced tomato, onion, jalapeño, and avocado), lifted the plastic, and forked out five slices of raw jalapeño.

Five? And with the seeds still intact? No way! I thought to myself, but said, "Ah, you're so sweet. Making me snacks and things."

"Here. No other food or drink for five minutes," he said, handing me the chips stacked high with jalapeños.

"Of course not. I want to savor the flavor," I said, and stuffed the loaded chips into my mouth.

Jalen shifted his bucket hat back on his head and watched me chew, smiling.

I smiled back, even as the heat grew so intense it made my eyes water.

He laughed.

Tears rolled down my cheeks, and I kept smiling and chewing.

Jalen laughed louder.

Forget this. I swallowed, got up, and ran toward the red cooler on the side of the house, near the barbeque pit, where Daddy and Mr. Wilson stood loudly debating LeBron.

"Oh no, you don't," Jalen shouted, chasing after me.

I swung the cooler's white top open. Cans of Big Red on ice smiled up at me. I could almost taste their cold, bubbly sweetness. But before I could reach in for one, Jalen pushed the top closed.

"Nah, homie."

I took off running again, this time to the back of the house, hoping to get to the hose before him. I didn't. So I kept running. Around the house, up the porch steps, past Mom and Mr. Wilson's girlfriend sitting in the chairs overlooking the lake, through the screen door, and into the house, where I headed for the kitchen sink.

Jalen was on my heels.

I turned on the faucet and stretched my neck and tongue toward the running water.

The water stopped. "You still have three minutes," he

said, laughing, with his hand on the lever, hunched over me from behind.

I began to turn around and he let go. "You went swimming earlier and didn't shower," I said, bringing my nose close to his neck to take in more of the sun and earth and sweat I smelled. It made me miss the lake.

He backed up, looking half surprised and half something I didn't recognize, which was weird but I didn't have time to think about it.

I ran out the back door and headed for the trees. My mouth had started to calm down, but I didn't want the game to end.

As I ran up the hill into the woods, a lizard dashed over my feet. No Jalen behind me, I slowed down and caught my breath. The smell of damp earth still hung in the air from the much-needed rain that morning, and I breathed it in deep, listening for footsteps behind me. None, so I slowed down even more.

A familiar song filled the air. High-pitched and vibratory like a whistle—*a-rree, a-rree, a-rree.* I looked up in the trees but couldn't find the bird it belonged to. The singing continued, and I wished I still knew how to name birds by their songs. Gigi had taught me countless birdsongs and many other things about life in the woods, but I'd forgotten so much.

I pushed a small branch out of my way and sprinkles of water fell on my nose and shoulders from high above. I opened my mouth, tipped my head back, pushed a different branch, and waited for more cool sprinkles to land on my hot, dry tongue.

A hand slid above my face. "Don't even try it."

I laughed and turned around, wondering how Jalen had snuck up on me. I was about to take off running again when he placed a finger to his mouth and pointed to some deer a little farther up the hill.

Slowly we walked closer and crouched down together beside a large tree to watch them.

"Wait, is that Blackberry?" Jalen quietly asked after a minute or so. "Man, I haven't seen her over here in forever."

"Blackberry?" I asked in a hush voice.

"Yeah, you see the doe munching on the dogweed?"

"Mm-hm."

"Well, when she was a fawn, she used to come steal black-berries off the bushes near our front porch. Her mama never came that close. Wouldn't risk it. But Blackberry must've thought those berries were extra good because she didn't even scare off when I'd come outside to go to the lake. Would just look up at me and go right back to eating. Greedy butt," he whispered, grinning.

I stared at him. His shining face. At how happy he was to see the deer. To have the memories. And I thought about how memories were such a weird thing. Saving themselves up inside us, waiting to come alive again.

"Can you see that black mark in the middle of her forehead shaped like a blackberry?"

"Yeah," I whispered, staring at the large dark patch between her eyes.

"Funny, right? I used to look forward to catching her munching in our yard, but soon after she lost all her spots, she stopped coming around. I guess she found someone else's berries to chew on."

"Aww," I sighed playfully.

Jalen smiled and poked out his bottom lip.

"But she came back to you," I whispered dramatically and looked up at her. She was putting her foot down on a fawn's neck. "Ouch."

"Dang, Blackberry. I know you gotta teach the youngster about herd hierarchy and all, but is that necessary?" Jalen said quietly. Then he turned to me and added, "It was probably trying to steal some of her food."

I laughed, a little too loud; and Blackberry looked up, alert ears forward, and ran off. The other deer followed.

After that, we pressed ourselves up and continued to the top of the hill, which wasn't too much higher.

At the summit, sky met trees and lake and stretched for miles around, making me feel big and small at the same time. Like I was a part of it all, as Gigi used to always say. I tipped my face up toward the bright, cloudy sky and closed my eyes, feeling a strong breeze press against my body. Everything inside me went quiet.

"Remember this?" Jalen asked, unknowingly interrupting the moment.

I opened my eyes and turned around. He was sitting on a small flat boulder, looking at something.

Before I even walked over, I remembered.

J + E
FOREVER

The black paint had faded, but after all these years it was still there. I ran my hand over the letters, remembering my last day in Alula Lake.

I'd just finished painting another portrait of Jalen. I liked painting him up here because of the view and because it wasn't too far from the house. Anyway, afterward we climbed up onto this boulder and stared out at the wide lake below, at the blue sky above, at the tree-covered hills holding foxes and birds and deer we couldn't see.

"Don't you wish summer could last forever?" he'd asked.

"Yeah, and we could be free to do what we want and not have homework or school."

"And you'd always be here."

"Yeah, that would be so cool," I'd replied. Then we linked hands. In gladness. In love. Not the romantic kind, but the love of swimming and racing and playing together. The love of grilled cheese sandwiches—mine with grape jelly and his with the crust cut off. The love of finding fossilized sand dollars and gastropods along the shore from millions of years ago. Of being artist and subject . . . captain and passenger. Of our time together.

I'd dipped my paintbrush in what seemed the most enduring color and wrote "*J + E*" in big black letters on top of the boulder. Then Jalen took the brush from me and wrote "*FOREVER.*"

The memory took me by surprise, and I wondered where it had been.

"What are you thinking about?" Jalen asked from up on the rock.

"Nothing," I answered, still halfway down memory lane, twirling my hair. Not something I usually did, but I'd unconsciously pulled at a small section of my hair and was winding the wavy strands around my finger. When I noticed, I stopped and gazed up at Jalen, hoping he hadn't seen me. But the funny look on his face told me he had.

For a second we stared at each other, a strange softness thickening around us until the wind blew through again, bending the trees, rustling the leaves, and stirring us up.

"Anyway, you hungry?" Jalen asked, hopping down from the rock.

"Starving," I answered, and we headed back.

Chapter 16

*T*he next morning was a Saturday, and I woke up feeling like I could finally trust myself enough to call Justine without sounding pathetic.

"So, why didn't you get his number? He could've definitely helped get your mind off Miles," she said, the sound of her wooden blinds clacking together coming through the phone. I imagined looking out of her bedroom window at the sun shining down on the swan floaties in her pool. Shining down on Houston. On its pine trees, shopping strips, and manicured lawns.

"First of all, the only time I think about Miles is when y'all bring him up," I lied. I picked up a T-shirt and sniffed the pits (my primary way of deciding if something was clean or dirty). I was straightening up my room. "And secondly, I wasn't about to ask for Craig's number with Jalen right there."

"So, you're not allowed to get numbers in front of Jalen?"

Clearly I hadn't relayed the part of the story where I ghosted him well enough. "It's not even like that. Plus, my phone was messed up from getting wet."

"Girl, you better learn to put your memorization skills to work."

I was beginning to wish I hadn't told her the story. It wasn't about Craig. Well, it was, but it was more about the lake. About how much I'd missed it. How alive it had made me feel. How the newness of speeding across the top of it had made me forget about all my problems and lose my sense of time. Lose myself, which somehow made me feel like I was getting closer to myself.

But I hadn't told her any of that. I hadn't told anybody. I'd carried it around for weeks only to have it come out as ordinary boy chat.

"You should've made his number into a song like I did yesterday when we were at the mall."

I assumed "we" meant her, Dani, and Cara. The mall was cool and all, but those three acted like there weren't better places to go. Dani and Cara always used the excuse of needing inspiration for their fashion designs. But Justine was in the vocal music program, so she didn't have an excuse. She just liked the boys and snacks.

"Threee, four-six, two-threee. Eight, five, nine, sev-en," she sang to the tune of Bob Marley's "No Woman, No Cry." "Ha! See, I still remember it!"

I laughed and threw a sundress with barbeque stains in the dirty pile. "None of y'all had your phones?"

"No," she said as if I was wrong for asking, "you know we're doing that phone cleanse."

"Phone cleanse?" I asked, doubting I'd ever feel like a part of their group again.

"We didn't tell you about it?"

"Nah."

"My bad. Well, my therapist suggested I stay off social for a month to see if it helps with my anxiety. But with my phone constantly yelling at me to check it, I figured out early that the easiest thing would be to avoid having it with me altogether. Cara and Dani are doing it, too. You wanna try? I'm not gon' lie, it feels super-weird for the first week, but it gets easier. Now I love it. It frees up so much time. You should hear the songs I've been writing. And oh my God. Cara designed this tweed jumpsuit that you would freakin' love."

"Really? Sounds cool. I don't know if I could live without my phone, though," I said, thinking about all the hours I wasted looking at TikTok videos while Jalen was at Stevie's. Hours I could've been painting or at least trying to paint.

"No pressure or anything. You've never been the anxious type. And it sounds like your summer has been fabulous, so you probably don't feel the need."

It wasn't true, and I wanted to tell her. But I didn't know how to share what was really going on with me without sounding like I needed her sympathy, so I said, "But I'm happy for y'all, though. Maybe I'll try it someday."

A serious of rhythmic taps at my window.

"Oh, that's Jalen. I gotta go," I said, relieved to be rescued from my own fakeness.

"Dang, this early?"

I looked over my shoulder through my cream sheers and saw Jalen, his shadowy figure almost like an angel. "Yeah, I told you we run down to the lake together every morning."

"Mm-hm."

I knew what that sound meant. She was thinking the thing I had scrubbed my mind clean of the night before. The thing that I was determined not to think. Yet her thinking it made me think it, which sent a strange surge of energy down my chest and into my belly, where it swam in dizzying circles.

"Just friends, huh?" she added suspiciously.

I couldn't take it. Her words were making my insides go crazy. I leaned over and picked up a dust ball full of my hair in a corner of my room. Holding it in my palm, I imagined taking it into my mouth and swallowing it—my long, coarse strands struggling down my throat, the bitter filth on my tongue. The spinning stopped.

"Yes. *Just* friends," I finally said. "Jalen is like a brother to me. No way that would ever happen." And before she could respond, I added, "Anywho, gotta go. I'll call you later. Bye!" and hung up the phone.

Chapter 17

I had no idea what I was after. Frantically pressing my paintbrush to canvas. Twisting it. Turning it. Moving the round tip over thick blue paint. There were gobs of it. Each stroke sending the acrylic in a different direction. Creating new shapes. Getting closer to something. But what? I didn't know.

I'd been painting since I'd gotten back from the lake, where I'd sat in the shade of a tree and watched Jalen help a little girl overcome her fear of swimming. Watched as he took her hand and slowly guided her into the water while her mother looked on from the rocky shore. Watched as he invited her to play, to slap the water so hard that it splashed back up in her face. As he placed his hands under her and showed her how easy it was to float on her back when she wasn't afraid.

It was the same way Gigi had taught kids to swim for years. Same way she'd taught me. And watching it filled me with things I had no words for, things I needed to paint.

With the sun spreading its last light around the studio, I lifted my brush off the canvas and stepped away from the easel to see what I'd been painting all day. A swirling mass of blue with stringy lines—orange, purple, green, and red—randomly strewn throughout, sometimes forming unrecognizable shapes. Then in thick black strokes, small circles inside of larger circles, a tiny row of circles. Even the blue background was a big, messy circle, a splotch of yellow in the center. And at the bottom, the last part I'd added, dark-blue strokes went round and round and through each other. Flew out and swooped in before heading out and then circling back into the dark-blue blob.

Each stroke had felt so urgent, but I didn't know what any of them meant. I sat down on the cool concrete floor and stared at the painting as light left the sky, hoping to spot something that would help me see myself. When I didn't, I stretched out on the floor beside the easel, listening to the golden bells outside the window tinkle every now and then, until the room went dark.

A vibration on the wooden table above my head. I stood up to see a text from Jalen letting me know he was home from Stevie's. Then I spun the easel around to face the back window so that I could see my painting better in the glow of the outdoor floodlight.

It was a mess. I had no idea where it came from or what it meant. And it wasn't my self-portrait. But it filled me with more hope than I'd felt in months. I barely wanted to leave it but couldn't skip hanging out with Jalen. I hadn't in so long.

Sitting in a lawn chair on the back of the truck, looking out at the bright stars, I helped Jalen finish a bag of cheese puffs. As I licked the sticky orange dust off my fingers (trying to avoid the patches of dried paint), he offered me a napkin from the white plastic bag with "Thank You" stacked seven times in red block lettering. I took it, finished licking, and briefly wiped my damp fingers.

He cleaned his hands thoroughly before reaching for the bottle of lemonade between his legs. Then he took a sip and held it out to me. "You want the rest of this?"

"I don't want your backwash," I answered, eyeing the small remaining amount.

"It doesn't have any backwash."

"Of course it does."

"I'm telling you, it doesn't. I swear if I could test it in a lab, I could prove that this lemonade is ninety-nine-point-nine percent free of backwash."

I laughed. "What?"

"I'm serious. You know how much I used to hate seeing food floating in my drinks as a kid. I got sick of wasting good juice, fruit punch, and sun tea. So, I developed a technique to prevent anything escaping my mouth during sips."

"Oh my gosh," I said, rolling my eyes and laughing harder.

"For real, though. I always drink with my head tilted back. And after I finish, I make sure to close my lips before pulling the cup or bottle or whatever away from my mouth," he said this with a serious face. "The trick is sealing your lips before the flow reverses."

I threw myself forward in the lawn chair, cracking up. I was hysterical.

"Laugh all you want, but it works. No crumbs. No back-wash. So here," he said, and handed me the bottle. "Trust me. It's safe."

Behind Jalen, Lena, in a halter top, stepped out of the house into the porch light. I hadn't seen her in weeks.

I took a sip of the cold, sweet liquid and handed the bottle back to Jalen. Then, pinky to pointer, I started cleaning the cheese dust from underneath my fingernails with the napkin. When Lena got close, I stopped.

"You coming?" she asked, staring up at us from just beyond the truck's opened gate.

Come on, Jalen. Please! I begged internally while externally trying to fix my face to be nonchalant.

"That was a one-time thing," Jalen answered. "You know that's not my scene."

"I wasn't talking to you."

Wait, does that mean she's talking to me? My heart did a little dance but stilled when it occurred to me that this was not the plan. I was supposed to go back to The Cove with Jalen. And this time, I was supposed do the right thing: let him know before I went off on the Jet Ski and not stay too long out on the lake. Maybe even get Craig to invite him to come along on the other Jet Ski. I wasn't prepared for Lena to ask me to come alone.

"You should go," Jalen said, trying to make it easy for me.

"Yeah?"

"Yeah," he repeated.

Lena turned and walked off toward the car waiting at the bottom of the hill.

I hopped off the truck. "You sure?" I asked again.

"She's about to leave you," he said.

I looked down the hill, feeling guilty. Then I balled up my napkin and threw it at Jalen playfully. It hit him in the chest.

"I don't want your trash!" He laughed and acted like he was going to throw it back.

"Too bad!" I yelled, and rushed to catch up with Lena.

What She Missed

Jalen opening his mouth to call her back and then closing it. Not for his sake. For hers. He knew she was struggling, searching, and that Lena didn't have the answers. But he also knew that Indigo was smart. She used to know this, but it seemed like she didn't anymore. Just like she no longer knew that swimming in the lake was good for her. She was trippin' but he had to let her go. He had to trust that in her own way, in her own time, she would again come to know what she needed to know.

Chapter
18

It wasn't the wind filling my T-shirt that made me think it was going to be a good night. Or my untwisted hair flying in a hundred directions at once. Or the radio blasting some rock band I didn't know. Or the chunk of dislodged cheese puff that rolled over my tongue.

It wasn't even how Lena caught me staring at the five inked birds flying over her left shoulder and shot me a quick smile. Or how her and Rebecca kept firing incomprehensible lyrics and pointed fingers up at the sky like they were giving it a piece of their minds.

It was how their energy spread to me. How it made me stick my arm out the window and pump my fist. And when that didn't feel like enough, take off my seat belt, stand up through the sunroof—half my body lost to the night—and yell at the darkness like I owned it. Until my cheeks went numb and I choked on too much wind and had to sit my butt back down, coughing and laughing.

Lena laughed with me, looking back in surprise and admiration, making me feel like I'd finally won her. "I knew you were nothing like Jalen," she shouted over the music.

"What?" I shouted back, not knowing how else to respond.

She turned down the radio, repeated herself, and added, "Always walking around with a stick up his ass."

Her words snatched the spirit out of me, and I imagined pulling Jalen in close. I could almost hear him beside me still talking about his backwash-prevention technique. I started cracking up.

Lena misinterpreted my laugh and turned to Rebecca. "See, told you. She's just with him all the time because he's her only friend here."

Rebecca briefly glanced at Lena and kept bobbing her head to the electric guitar still playing softly on the radio.

Lena turned back toward me, pulling her seat belt away from her neck. "I would've invited you to hang sooner but you stopped coming over. At first I thought maybe you went back to Houston for a bit, but then I overheard Jalen on the phone with Adrick and Quentin talking about how you were trippin'. It's obvious why y'all fell out. He got mad at you for going on the Jet Ski, didn't he?"

I nodded, surprised by how much attention she paid to me and that she talked so much.

She turned to Rebecca again. "See." Then she shook her head and turned back to me, "Only Jalen would get mad at somebody for having fun at a party. That's when I really knew I needed to rescue you."

Looking out of the window at a shopping strip I'd never seen before, with a bakery, pet inn, and UPS, I tried to think of a way to tell her that she was wrong. That I had been wrong. That her brother was hilarious and my favorite person to be around. But I knew her terms. If I was going to hang with her, I'd have to hate on Jalen. "Oh my God. You don't even know how bad I've been wanting to escape. All Jalen ever wants to do is go to the lake and sit on the back of his stupid pickup truck," I said, heat flashing up my cheeks.

"Don't worry. I gotcha, boo," she said, apparently satisfied, and turned the music back up.

We rode about five more minutes in the blast of strings and drums, past new businesses, construction sites, and big houses until we took a right and the trees got thick and dark again. And it felt like the real Alula Lake. The one I'd always known, with a country road winding back and forth up a hill to a gravel parking lot.

Stepping out of the car, I squinted underneath the bright lamppost. The air, warm and scented with smoke, stirred the energy inside me. I was ready to join the party again. But as I ran behind Lena and Rebecca down the wooden staircase between the cabins to the beach, I didn't hear music. I didn't see anyone dancing or throwing a football. There was no table with bags of chips or red plastic cups.

Only Craig.

Shirtless in the light of the fire. Back flexed from carrying a large bundle of wood. He dropped the branches outside the edge of the fire pit. Then he grabbed one of the larger branches, placed it on top of the fire, and shot the whole thing with a few squirts of lighter fluid. Flames shot up.

"Ah, yeah. Ah, yeah," Lena yelled, halfway across the narrow beach.

Craig turned around, pushed his short locs out of his face, and shouted, "Y'all took forever!"

"You know we had to wait for Jalen to get back," Lena said. "Plus, we brought you a friend."

All eyes were on me, and I resisted looking down at the tiny rocks and shells shifting beneath my steps.

"You sure she can hang?" he tried to whisper, but the bass in his voice betrayed him.

I wondered what the deal was.

Lena looked at Rebecca and said, "Is he serious right now?"

Then she turned to Craig and said, "Are you really up here acting like you haven't been talking our ears off about this girl for the last two weeks?" She laughed and continued, "Indigo this. Indigo that. I couldn't take it anymore, so I brought her along."

For a millisecond, his eyes widened in shock. But he played it cool and watched me as I walked up to the half circle they'd formed. His face opened into a bright-eyed smile. "Hey."

I couldn't help but grin back, flashing my gap. "Hey."

"Your hair is different."

"Yeah, I untwisted it a few days ago," I replied, happy he noticed.

"Looks cool."

"Well, it probably looks crazy from the ride over here but thanks."

"Nah, maybe a little wild, but it looks good like that."

Rebecca was done listening to whatever was going on between us. "So, is everybody ready?" she asked, the high cheekbones on her small face shining in the glow of fire.

Ready for what? I asked internally.

"Yeah, let's be out," Craig replied.

A bubble of uneasiness rose inside me. And here came Jalen again, feeling impossibly close, telling me to act like I had good sense. Telling me to find out where we were going and what we'd be doing.

But the thing he didn't understand was that I'd been sensible my whole life and felt like it had gotten me nowhere. That night on the Jet Ski with Craig was the first time I'd completely abandoned sense and let myself go. Maybe even the first time in my life that I'd truly felt free.

The thing Jalen could never know was that even with all the strain that night had put on our friendship, I'd been dreaming about it since.

Chapter 19

*C*raig smelled the same way he had the last time I'd had my arms and legs wrapped around him, like sweat and sweet cologne. The sky above was ablaze with the same stars. The same engine roared beneath me. The same wind pressed against my face and whirled in my ears. The dark hills, once again, presided over everything.

But it felt better than the first time.

We didn't even zigzag or do doughnuts or cross our own wake. We zipped over the lake in a straight line behind Lena and Rebecca, the anticipation of what was to come sending chills up my spine.

Then ahead, a neon blue sign that read "Stevie's." We slowed down and headed toward the empty slip beside the other Jet Ski.

"Stevie's is still open?" I asked, knowing Jalen closed the shop up at seven thirty every night.

"No, but don't worry. Lena has the keys," Craig assured me. We both watched as she walked up to the back door of the trailer, unlocked it, and disappeared inside.

A terrible feeling began to stir in my stomach. Then Jalen slid in close to me, again, this time with no words, face blooming with disappointment.

I could've told Craig, *I can't get down with this. Take me back*. But I didn't. I pushed Jalen away and stepped off the Jet Ski onto the dock.

Until that moment, I'd thought I at least knew what kind of person I was. What I was or wasn't capable of. What I thought was right or wrong. Good or bad. But it was like a huge tide came in, covered my sixteen years, and drowned the basic things I thought I knew about myself.

The rest of the night, I tried not to think so I can't remember everything. I remember getting off the Jet Ski and pulling at the bottoms of my wet jean shorts every two seconds to keep them from sticking to my crotch. I remember seeing Rebecca in her bikini and her smiling at me when she caught me staring at her big boobs. I don't remember Lena coming back with the keys or taking my clothes off or even getting on the boat. But I do remember looking over at Craig with his hands on the same silver steering wheel Jalen had driven a couple weeks earlier and yelling, "Faster" in my panties and bra.

"Woooooo!" I screamed, looking back at Rebecca and Lena through my wild hair. They were wearing the same halter front-tie bikini in different colors, Lena's black and Rebecca's hot pink. Like their matching buzz cuts, Lena's reddish brown and Rebecca's blond. And their chokers, Lena's black leather and Rebecca's jute with beads. And their nose rings, Lena's a hoop and Rebecca's a stud. I hated friend groups who walked around looking like they all got the same style memo, and I delighted in finally feeling equal enough to judge them.

After doing a few tricks and going so fast my body felt like it might be permanently glued to the seat, Craig slowed all the way down and said, "Who's next?"

"Me," Lena said. She stood up and switched seats with him.

Then me and Rebecca got up and switched seats, too. I don't know why except that we'd been in the same pairs since we'd left The Cove and it felt right to keep it that way.

Lena went even faster than Craig, but was way less steady,

yanking the boat this way and that. She took a sharp turn and I held on to the metal railing, terrified the boat would tip over.

"Bro!" Craig yelled but she didn't seem fazed. Hand on the throttle, she sped out of the turn like she had something to prove.

Whole body stiff, I hooked my eyes on the gibbous moon and tried to let myself go. No, no, then finally, yes, and I threw my free hand in the air, riding the rough waters as if they were a giant roller coaster. When Lena finally slowed down, I laughed so hard I could barely catch my breath.

"That was crazy!" I shouted.

"Nah," Craig replied, looking at Lena. "You know, the boat *can* capsize. We *can* get thrown off. I've seen some serious lake accidents over the years and people *do* get hurt." He was heated.

Lena whipped her head around to face Craig. "Goodness. Nobody told me Jalen was gonna be on the boat."

"Look," he said in a more even tone. "I told you I was cool taking the boat out and showing you some tricks or whatever. But I'm not trying to deal with an accident. My uncle would flip, my parents would be pissed, and I would kiss my freedom goodbye."

"We've been coming out here having fun for almost two

weeks. Don't turn into a pussy now," Lena yelled.

"All I'm saying is that we have to stay in control," he replied firmly. "And 'pussy'? Isn't that sexist or something."

Lena stood up. "So, now you're out here trying to be the word police, too? Man, get on somewhere with all of that." She looked at Rebecca. "Your turn."

"Nah, I'm cool."

"Look, I didn't mean to discourage you," Craig told Rebecca, leaning toward her. He pushed his locs out of his face. "I just want to make sure—"

"It's not even like that. I've had my fill of driving, that's all. Now I'm trying to sit back and chill."

"I'll go," I said and we all played musical chairs again.

The driver's seat felt wet and cool beneath my cotton underwear. Uncomfortable with the secret pleasure, I shifted my butt around a few times before pushing the throttle forward. The engine growled underneath me, and the nose of the boat lifted. I couldn't see anything over it and freaked out.

No way I can do this, I told myself, letting up on the throttle. There was too much power in my hands. Too much I didn't understand about the dark waters. Drive a boat? It had barely been three months since I'd gotten my license to drive a car. And I hadn't even spent much time doing that after Mom sold her BMW and we went down to one vehicle.

"You're okay," Craig said, turning in his seat to face me. "You just need to go faster so the nose will lower."

"Faster?" I asked, doubting speed could be the remedy.

"Yeah, trust me."

For a few seconds, I debated abandoning the driver's seat, but it would've felt too embarrassing and defeating. So I pressed the throttle forward. More. Even more until the nose lowered and I regained visibility.

Fingers gripping the steering wheel, I didn't risk turning left or right. But I was driving a boat. Slamming into black wave after black wave, still on top. I went even faster in a straight line until the water smoothed out.

After a while, exhilaration spread over my fear and I took a wide turn, cool water splashing my face and arm.

"Woo," Lena and Rebecca yelled behind me.

I took another turn, the water parting beneath me, the wake leaving white lines in the dark. More turns, more marks, almost like brushstrokes. But I didn't have to decide what they meant because after a few seconds, they were gone. It felt like magic. Turn after turn and the shadowy trees seemed to tilt their crowns in for a closer look. A three-sixty and the bright stars clapped their tiny hands in applause.

I kept driving until I eventually had to return the steering wheel to Craig so that he could pull up beside the fuel dock at Ernie's, where he filled the boat up before taking it back. Sweet whiffs of gas, and I was already dreaming about doing it all again.

Walking as soft-footed as I could across the rocks alongside the house, preparing to quietly slip in through the back door, I noticed something taped to my bedroom window. A wrinkled napkin with a fat, black, downward-facing arrow. I looked on the ground below and saw my phone propped up against the house. I must've left it on the truck.

I grabbed it, peeled the tape off the window, and went inside. Safely behind the closed door of my room, I turned on the lights and looked at the napkin again.

On the back, there was Jalen's neat, squished handwriting scrawled over orange creases, smudges, and specks of dust:

Your phone and your trash. 😊
Hope you had a good night.

A whirlwind of guilt pulled me into its center, and I buried my face in the napkin, wondering if I'd ever feel like a good person again. I fought my way out by convincing myself that there was no harm done because we returned the boat in the same shape we'd found it. Then I took off my wet clothes, turned off the lights, and got under the comforter without covering my hair or brushing my teeth.

I wrapped myself in the simplest memories I could find. Jalen and I swimming and playing along the shore when we were young. It felt so comforting, like climbing into old skin. Memory after memory until I finally fell asleep.

Chapter
20

*T*he next morning when Jalen came to get me to race down to the lake, I slid open my bedroom window, rubbed the crust out of my eyes, and told him I was too sleepy. Plus, did he see my hair? It would take all day to wash, detangle, and retwist.

The day after that, I told him about how Daddy had been looking for his flathead screwdriver and when he couldn't find it had bought a new one. Then of course he found the old one. I needed to return the new one to the store for him that morning so he and Mom could have breakfast together before he went to the jobsite.

The day after that, it was crucial that I restore this photo of Gigi I'd found in the junk drawer while looking for a flashlight. The photo was beautiful. He should see it. She was young and standing in a vegetable garden. But the print was wrinkled and faded. I needed to use the morning to Photoshop it back to life.

Things went on like that for a few more days until the morning I was waiting for Justine to FaceTime.

"You know the boy I told you she picked up at the mall?" I asked Jalen. He was standing outside my window in front of a bright blue sky streaked with thin clouds.

He didn't respond. He just stood there, eyes piercing mine from underneath his bucket cap.

I continued, upbeat, like I didn't notice the way he was looking at me. "Well, they're about to go on their first date to the Breakfast Klub, which is a very big deal. Not only because brunch dates are the cutest, but because he chose a see-and-be-seen place. That means he must really like her. So, she wants to FaceTime me, Cara, and Dani to get our advice on some outfits in a bit."

"So, I guess now that you're hanging with Lena, you don't have time for me anymore, huh?" Jalen replied, balancing his directness with a playful smile.

I didn't know to deal with his honesty, so I played dumb. "What are you talking about?"

He lost his smile. "Really, Indigo?"

"What? I see you every night," I said, idiotically doubling down.

"Barely. You come over for, like, five minutes before Lena comes out. Then you're gone."

"I don't know. I mean, half the time when you text me that you're back from Stevie's, I'm in the middle of doing something. Then by the time I get over there, Lena's ready to go."

He laughed under his breath. "You know what? Don't worry about it."

I looked into his eyes and silently begged for forgiveness. I missed him, too. But hanging out with him and then stealing the boat night after night didn't work. It made me feel gross, like someone I didn't want to be.

"I'll try to come a little earlier tonight," I told him.

He pulled a face like I'd just offered him a glass of juice with crumbs floating in it. "I'm good," he said, and walked off.

"But I want to," I called after him.

He didn't reply.

An ache swelled at the base of my throat. I couldn't lose him again. I thought about shouting, *Wait*, running to catch up, and confessing everything. But the anticipation of taking the boat out that night wouldn't let the truth approach my lips.

"Oh, I almost forgot," he yelled, turning around.

I let out a long breath.

"Genesis wants your help tomorrow."

I hated hearing her name but couldn't waste the chance of having the conversation with Jalen end on a better note. I sat on the windowsill, swung my legs over, and walked barefoot over the spiky rocks toward him. I half hoped he'd tell me to put some shoes on or watch out for scorpions, but he didn't.

"Help doing what?" I asked, already enjoying the idea of saying no.

"Painting a mural for Homecoming down at the church."

The simple goodness of what she needed my help with pissed me off. I couldn't say no. Not to Homecoming. Not after watching Gigi create art for it all those years. Not after listening to her talk about all the food her mother would cook for it. Sweet potatoes and collard greens from her own garden. Chickens and turkeys from her own flock. Or how her great-grandmother, a pastor's wife, started the tradition to celebrate the town's history. It would've felt like I was saying no to Gigi and all my ancestors. Still, I wanted to. "Oh, that sounds amazing," I lied.

"Cool, I told her that you'd probably need a ride," he

said, squinting into the sun. "She said she'd come scoop you. I gave her your number so y'all could work it out."

I started to tell him that I didn't want to get in a car with that annoying girl, but we had already exceeded the day's limit for strained conversation. I shoved the words back down my throat. "Tomorrow is Thursday. Don't you have it off? Can you take me? Maybe stay? Please? I mean, she's your friend. I don't even know her like that."

A pause and then, "Fine."

"Thanks!" I said, and hugged him, mostly because I missed him.

He squeezed me back, lifting my feet off the ground. Then he grabbed me by my waist, threw me over his shoulder, and ran me back to my opened window.

I squealed and laughed the whole bumpy ride, trying to ignore the heat where his strong hands held on to the back of my thighs.

"You know you can't be coming out here with no shoes on," he said, putting me down.

"I know," I replied, staring at a bead of sweat traveling down the right side of his neck.

He backed away from the window. "They might not have bones, but they do have stingers."

"What?"

"Scorpions," he said, like, *Come on. Keep up.*

"Yeah, they're exoskeletons. Their skeleton is on the outside," I said, getting it together. I remembered studying scorpions for a series of sketches I did on crustaceans and arachnids for science class. We were allowed to incorporate art in nearly all our assignments at my old school.

"Well, one got me coming out of the shower last week and it was not fun," he said, still walking backward.

"Rude!"

"Gon' get you, too, if you keep coming out here with no shoes."

"Nah, I'm hard. I have an exoskeleton of my own!" I said jokingly, but I liked the idea of it.

"Keep believing that if you want to!" he said, laughing, and ran off into the woods.

Chapter 21

*L*ater that morning I worked up enough nerve to paint myself. I didn't want to continue with my old self-portrait, and I only had one clean canvas left, so I used the box that Mom's new headscarves had come in. If it turned out good, Mr. Marshall would appreciate the use of recycled material.

Sitting on a stool, I stared at the blank brown cardboard on the easel, not sure how to begin. Using a mirror was out of the question. The face looking back at me hadn't felt right since I'd started stealing the boat. It was like no matter what color eyeliner I put on, which way I styled my twists, or how glossy my lips were, the girl in the mirror was always looking at me funny. So, I had to find another route.

I tried scrolling through my phone for an old photo of

myself but was bombarded with what seemed like a hundred pictures of Jalen standing in front of a pink-and-purple sky. I stared at the way he gave himself up to the camera and imagined he was giving himself to me. Flustered, I turned off my phone.

Then I thought about how I'd actually liked the face on my old self-portrait. Until I realized my smile didn't match my eyes, got mad, and painted over it. I decided to re-attempt, this time ditching the smile, which was fake anyway.

I tried to remember which browns I'd used for the color of my skin, but I couldn't. So, I created a different palette for a slightly new version of me. A real one, with deep brown ochre, raw sienna, phthalo blue, cool yellow, and carmine lake red just because I liked the name.

But after spending nearly two hours sketching my face from memory and mixing paints for the tones of my skin, I ran into a problem. My head was facing straight ahead, but I didn't want my eyes to be because I didn't want them looking at me.

My chest throbbed. *Why?* I screamed inside myself. *Why does everything have to be so hard?*

I stared into the blank almond shapes I'd drawn as placeholders for my eyes, trying to imagine them looking back at me in peace. But I couldn't. And the longer I tried, the more they seemed to be glaring at me.

What the hell are you looking at? I demanded before vowing to ignore them. Then I started laying down deep brown strokes on the sides of my face and neck. When I was done, I added highlights and moved on to my chin, but I could still feel the glare.

Annoyed but determined, I kept painting, stroke after stroke, until my self-portrait started to come to life. But the glare was getting stronger, and I couldn't continue.

I was stuck.

Pissed, I dreamed of throwing the whole thing into the fire pit. Imagined orange and red flames shooting up. Growing higher and higher until a fiery beast climbed out and started screaming at me.

Terrified, I tried to escape by working on the background. Blue, blue, and more blue to put out the flames. I decided the light would come from the left and added white as I moved to the right.

Better.

Waiting for the paint to dry, I stretched out on the concrete floor and tried to think good thoughts. Jalen carrying me over his shoulder earlier. I relived each bumpy step and let them transport me to the piggyback rides he always gave me when we were kids. Even my first summer in Alula Lake, when he was shorter than me. When he still had a slight lisp and I missed Mom so much that I cried all the time.

I stood up and looked at my self-portrait. The background was dry, but I had the same problems I had earlier. The eyes, the annoyance, the flames, the same beast yelling something at me. *What?* I was too afraid to find out. So I kept painting to extinguish the flames. Blue upon blue upon blue until I was the girl with no face again.

I had to get away from her.

I ran out of the studio and into the woods. It had been a week since I'd raced to the lake with Jalen, and my lungs burned. But I kept running down the path, the faceless girl fading with every step.

Legs in a rhythm, my attention turned to the woods around me. I'd missed the cedar smell. Missed the birds, wildflowers, squirrels, and deer. The bits of sun shining down through the cozy cover of green leaves and making patterns on the earth. The twisted trunks of the old junipers and the long, curvy branches of the live oaks. The trees didn't reach high to the sky like Houston's pines, but their beauty still made something good rise in me.

The good attracted more good and convinced me that this would be the day I finally got into the lake. I was tired of being afraid. I wanted to cool off. Maybe swim out to the lighthouse. Or at least float on my back with my eyes closed, my favorite thing to do as a child.

As soon as I got to the edge of the woods and saw the lake, I stopped. It looked so grand and glorious under the bright blue sky. So different than the wild and dangerous vibes it gave me on the boat at night. I stood there for a minute taking it in before I leaped down and sprinted across the shore.

"Hello, lake," I sang as I kicked off my sneakers at the water's edge. The words felt so good that they seemed to vibrate on my tongue. Entranced, I repeated, "Hello, lake," but this time, it felt more like I was saying the wrong lyrics to an old song. Staring down at the small, foamy waves running toward my long, skinny toes, then pulling away, I tried to remember the right words but couldn't.

I inched my toes closer to the water, but when a wave surprised me and rushed at my feet, I yelped and ran back. I did this a few times, pretending to play a game.

But it wasn't fun. I was already sweaty from the run, and the longer I stood there with the high sun beating down on me, the hotter I became.

Get in, I told myself.

I didn't want to be afraid of the lake.

Get in now, I demanded.

I didn't want this to be the place I kept picturing Gigi's dead body.

Come on!

I wanted to swim in the lake and love it again.

This is your last chance! Get in now or I'm never coming back here! I threatened myself.

But I still couldn't do it. Feeling stupid and weak, I stared at the water until tears welled up in my eyes.

I swear I hate you, I growled at myself before running back up the hill.

Chapter 22

*T*he second time I saw Genesis was even worse than the first. She was alone, wearing white overalls and a tank top—disgustingly cute—working on the almost-finished mural on the side of the church. Even more crushing, the mural was so stunning it made my head go light as my eyes tried to take it all in at once.

There was the lighthouse overlooking the lake, horses, waves, a cluster of three children, waves, a boat, birds in flight, a cowboy hat, stars, waves, a woman with a microphone, shells, waves, wildflowers, a bible, a man with an afro pick planted in the swirls atop his head, flames, and a kite with a cross—all flowing together in so many colors. At the mural's center, in black-and-white, the founders of

Alula Lake, a woman and two men with beards, looked out at everything. And "A Freedom Colony" painted in bright turquoise block letters across the bottom held it all up.

"I thought you said Genesis was a photographer," I said to Jalen, and rubbed my glossy lips together. We'd just gotten out of the truck and were walking across the church lawn.

"Yeah, that's her main thing. But you know how artists are. She paints, too."

His nonchalance made me want to plant my foot in the mound I was stepping over, let the fire ants run up my bare leg, and scream. Maybe then he'd ask himself how he forgot to tell me this very important detail . . . and if it looked like she needed my help . . . or if maybe inviting me here was her sick and twisted way of letting me know she was better (way, way better) than me at my thing.

She saw us and shouted, "Hey!" waving enthusiastically.

I covered my intimidation with a big smile and waved back. "Hey!"

Jalen briefly held a hand up, too. "Plus, there's no way her mom would've let her get out of helping. Mrs. Williams is the one in charge of this whole thing. She designed it and sketched it. She usually has, like, thirty volunteers out here helping, mostly her students from school."

I instantly felt stupid for thinking Genesis could've done the mural on her own, especially with the dozens of paint cans on the drop cloth that stretched the whole length of the church. *She ain't nobody,* I told myself, pretending I was over being insecure around her.

"I don't know where they're at today, though."

"Who?"

"Mrs. Williams's students."

"Wait, Mrs. Williams who teaches art at Alula High?"

"Yeah, you know her?"

"I don't know her, know her. But my mom did Zumba with her one night at the gym and has been bugging me about calling her since."

"Why haven't you? She's mad cool. And an amazing artist, as you can—" We were walking under an old live oak, and he jumped up to tap one of its long arms. "See," he grunted upon landing.

"I don't know."

"But she could probably help you with that painting you have to hand in this summer. Have you been working on it?"

"No," I answered, annoyed at him for asking. It made me feel like I was coming apart.

"But isn't it due in, like—"

"Please," I said, looking dead at him to make him stop. Fiery tears raced toward the backs of my eyes, and I quickly turned away.

"Sorry. I didn't—"

"Don't worry about it," I cut him off. We were getting close, and I needed to get myself together.

"I'm so glad y'all came," Genesis said as we approached, her T-zone shiny with sweat and happiness. She put her brush, covered with burnt-orange paint, down on top of one of the cans and gave Jalen a hug.

I did my best to act like I wasn't bothered by seeing her arms around him.

"Oh no," she said, looking at his white tee after pulling away. "I'm so sorry. I wasn't thinking."

Jalen looked down at the orange splotch on his shirt. "No big deal. I get these in packs of six at Walmart."

"Yeah, we're here to help paint. It was bound to happen," I said, and gave her a hug. Not because I wanted to, but because I needed to convince myself that I could do this. Spend the day painting with her and Jalen when they maybe had a thing. When that maybe-a-thing nudged the feelings that I'd convinced myself weren't real to swim up to the surface and do laps around my heart. When I was guilty, insecure, and on the verge of tears.

We both smiled as we pulled away from each other and saw the orange spot on my Nirvana T-shirt.

"I don't know any of their songs anyway," I said.

"Me, either," she replied. "And I have, like, three of their T-shirts. It's hard not to. They're—"

"Everywhere!" we said in unison, and laughed. In the moment it felt like we were real friends, but I doubted the feeling would last.

"Come on," she said, heading toward the back of the church through the parched, patchy grass. "My mom has been dying to meet you."

Inside, one of Gigi's huge plant-dyed canvases greeted me, along with the familiar smells of dusty bibles and wood polish. The canvas glowed orange, yellow, bronze, and pink, and hung staring at *God Is Love* in blues, violets, and greens on the opposite wall.

My heart swelled as I remembered Gigi painting the wall: double doors open and sunshine pouring in while Jalen and I played hide-and-seek all over the church. As I remembered her boiling the canvas in her black cauldron over the fire pit night after night to get the clusters of colors just right.

"I'll be back," Genesis said, and ran off, her sneakers squeaking on the waxy wood floors.

"Look at Mama G's work, still living on," Jalen said, standing beside me.

"Remember when you slipped and busted it on that plastic drop cloth?"

He laughed. "Man, my butt was sore for a week!"

"That's what you get. I don't know how many times Gigi told you to stop running in the church," I said in a mock-scolding tone.

"*Me?* I was chasing you!"

"Well, I'm not the one who fell," I said, and we both cracked up.

"Y'all made it," a woman's voice sang, and I turned to see an older, more goddess-like version of Genesis walking toward me in a flowy, strappy, black dress. Her eyes shone with the same happiness under her thick brows. Her middle-parted hair, streaked with grays, was tied back in a loose bun.

"Hi, Mrs. Williams," Jalen said.

"Hey. Stevie doesn't have you working today?"

"No, ma'am. I have Thursdays off."

"I'll have to remember that when I need volunteers," she

said playfully and turned her attention to me. "Good Lord, if you don't have your mother's face."

I smiled a real smile. Not because I was proud to look like Mom, but because there was no denying I did. We had the same high cheekbones, round nostrils, biggish lips, and forehead; the same long chin and small gap between our two front teeth. But since my skin was so much darker than hers, most people didn't see it. It was weird.

"She tells me you're an incredible painter," Mrs. Williams said, walking past me. She pushed the long silver bar on one of the back doors.

I squinted at the sun pouring in and followed her. "I don't know about all that."

"What do you mean?"

I shrugged without thinking and it brought me back to being in Houston, sitting on Ms. Kristi's tufted leather sofa, staring at the dead dragonfly on the table outside her window. Mondays and Thursdays for a whole month, that dragonfly pulled me into a daydream while I shrugged at Ms. Kristi's annoying questions. We'd fly off over her rosebushes, down University Boulevard, where we'd always make a stop on someone's ice cream before we lifted off and roamed around Rice Village until we got bored and rode the wind higher above the neighborhood, even higher above the whole city. Henry, I'd named him before the lawn guy carelessly blasted him away with a leaf blower and I convinced my parents that I was fine so I wouldn't have to go back.

"Your mom showed me some of your work. You're extremely talented. You must know that, right?"

"Yes," I said, feeling something in my chest click back into place.

"Good. Well, don't say stuff you don't mean. Especially not about yourself. It confuses things."

I didn't know exactly what she meant, but I looked at her and gratefully said, "Okay."

She walked across the dry grass to the drop cloth, squatted, and, using the wooden end of a brush, hammered an opened can's top back down. "As you can see, the mural is pretty much there," she said and pressed herself back up in her Birkenstocks. "But I left some places unfinished for people who want to take part."

A breeze moved through the grid on my scalp, and my eyes were drawn to a section of unfinished waves on the mural behind her. I could've sworn they rippled. "Thank you," I replied. "It's so beautiful. So special."

"Yeah, this is the preservation of history right here,"

Jalen added, walking up beside me. "It'll be so cool driving by it all the time and feeling like I had something to do with it. You're the best, Mrs. Williams."

Genesis stood there inflated with so much pride that I thought her rainbow-checked Vans might float off the ground.

"Well, I'll be out here another what, three? No, two and half weeks until Homecoming. Y'all are welcome to come back anytime."

We thanked her again and chose the parts of the mural we wanted to work on. Genesis continued with the three birds in flight. Jalen climbed a ladder to brighten up the lighthouse, and I made my way to the waves on the other end.

Holding a paint-dipped pointed brush in my hand, I took a deep breath in, feeling the yearning nervousness that always came before making the first stroke. Paintbrush to primed brick wall and a tiny ray of light beamed inside me, guiding my hand, calming my nerves. Another stroke, more light, and more calm. Another after another until I was swimming in tiny lights.

Thirty minutes went by. Or maybe an hour. I didn't know because I wasn't paying attention to anything outside of the deep-blue troughs, the white crests, and the light-blue spaces in between.

Until I heard a mixture of high-pitched and bass-filled laughter and looked over at Jalen and Genesis. He'd climbed down from the ladder and was in front of the mural, shuffling his feet left to right, right to left. She had a huge smear of red paint across the bib of her overalls and was threating him with the can of burnt-orange paint.

I glared at them as they played their game. Her pretending to be on the verge of throwing the whole can, and him pretending to think she'd do it despite his proximity to the mural.

All the tiny lights inside my body grew dim, and I began to suspect that this was her plan all along. For me to see them together. For me to observe firsthand his enjoyment of her shininess, good style, and meticulously laid baby hair. For me to think twice before getting any ideas.

Feeling real disappointment, real betrayal, I rubbed my lips together and congratulated myself on not being optimistic enough to think our friendship would last. Rubbed my lips together and thought of all the ways I could call her out of her name. When she looked at me, I'm not sure which form of *backstabbing bitch* she saw on my face, but she stopped their game.

What
She
Missed

The wind blowing in from the south and cooling her scalp again. The pencil-sketched waves on the wall in front of her. Rippling. Trying to persuade her to dive back in.

Chapter
23

A decomposing deer carcass on the side of the road, and I thought about my stint as a vegetarian. A whole six months last year without meat before giving in to a bite of Justine's In-N-Out burger. It was a wrap after that.

When we passed the deer, I imagined seeing a black patch on its forehead. Imagined getting out of the car and consoling Jalen, assuring him that Blackberry was in a better place. Hugging him before our cheeks kissed and our lips met.

"You okay?" Jalen asked, eyes ahead on the winding road.

You're a sicko, I scolded myself before replying, "Yeah."

He turned down the personal injury lawyer's rap commercial playing on the radio. "What's wrong? You've been acting funny since we were at the church."

"I'm just hungry," I replied, picking at the dried blue paint on my nails.

He glanced over at me. "Come on, Indigo."

"I miss home," I said, initially because it was the easiest thing to reach for, way easier than asking about Genesis. But when "home" formed in my mouth, it opened some kind of valve in my brain and images started to flood in. The tire swing in our front yard. The silver Lab next door always begging for a belly rub. The neighborhood's sidewalks busted from tree roots pushing through. The canopy of crowns that kept me cool. Dani's dirty black Honda. Cara's pink braces. Lunch every day with them on the school's green lawn.

"I can't even imagine."

"I lived there my whole life. Well, not counting my summers here, but that's different."

"Yeah."

"Then the next thing I knew, it was my last day of school and everyone was all up in my face telling me how much they'd miss me. Such a lie. I mean, I'm sure my friends miss me a little. But life goes on. I learned that after Gigi died."

"I get what you mean. After my mom left, people felt sorry for me, but their lives went on as usual."

I studied him for a second to make sure he was okay. His hat was off, and I could see that his baseline brightness hadn't dimmed, so I replied, "Yeah, it's like the world never stops. No matter what happens to anyone. No matter how bad."

"Unless it's Covid," he said, and laughed.

I smiled. "Ugh, don't even mention it. But, for real, it would take something absolutely terrible to happen to everyone in the world at the exact same time for it to, like, really stop."

"That sounds like the Apocalypse."

"Exactly. And nobody wants that."

All of the light left in the sky was straight ahead—deep blue fading to yellow then darkening to dusty peach. I stared at it and said, "So, I guess that settles it then. We're all in this life alone until everything comes to an end."

"But that's what friends are for," he said, glancing over.

"Even friends don't know what you're really feeling."

He looked at me and back at the road. He looked at me again and I finally met his eyes. They were so tender. "At least we can try to understand."

I suddenly felt afraid about being so open. Afraid of confessing that I hadn't slept well in months. That I had to actively stop myself from crying when no one was around. That I blamed my parents for losing their jobs and was jealous of my friends for being able to stay in their houses and still have money to shop. That I didn't recognize myself. That I was a joy-riding criminal and terrible friend, who had feelings for him but wasn't dumb and knew that he liked Genesis.

"And there was this boy," I finally said, my jumbled thoughts finding a soft place to land. Plus, I wanted him to know that he wasn't the only one who could like someone else.

"Oh, you had to leave your boyfriend, too? That's extra hard."

"He wasn't exactly my boyfriend. We never even kissed," I admitted, hating myself for being so honest. I couldn't help it with Jalen. "But it would've happened if I would've stayed. We'd been flirting for, like, two years."

"Two years?"

"It was a slow burn type of thing, okay," I tried to explain. "We became friends because we were both the only freshman and then one of a few sophomores in Mr. Marshall's advance painting class."

"Oh, so that's why you weren't getting your work done," Jalen said jokingly.

"It's not even like that," I replied, smiling. "Miles was

just as serious about painting as I was. We both used to stay after school all the time to work. Mr. Marshall would leave the studio open for us and after we finished, we'd drop the keys in his mailbox."

He took his eyes off the road to glare at me with playful suspicion. "So, you're telling me that y'all used to be up in the studio alone all the time but never kissed?"

Seeing "kiss" leave Jalen's lips sent a flash of lightening low through my belly and made my body feel hot. I cracked my window and said, "Well, we almost did."

"Almost how? Like what happened?"

"Oh, I see you're trying to get *all* up in the business."

"Of course I am," he said, a flirty grin taking over his face.

Could Jalen have feelings for me, too? I wondered. More bolts of lightning and I rolled my window down farther.

"Here, I can turn up the air," Jalen said, twisting the knob.

Cool air poured out of the vents, and I rolled my window up.

"Is that better?"

"Yeah."

"Okay, back to your business," he said, and laughed.

It was the same way he'd laughed since we were five—grinning, upper body quaking—but now it made me feel like I was about to pass out. "Fine," I said, pushing through because I figured he'd be up next, and I wanted all the details on him and Genesis. I took a deep breath. "It was the second-to-last day of school and we'd stayed after to work on our self-portraits. They were due the next day, and we were the only ones who hadn't turned them in. So, the studio was set up with everybody's easels and wooden stools in a circle, right?"

"Okaay," Jalen said, like he wished I would hurry up and get to the good part.

"Look, the details are important. Are you gonna let me tell the story or what?"

"All right, all right."

"Anyway, I was sitting at six o'clock and he was at ten, which gave me a good line of vision to look at him when I was frustrated with trying to paint myself. But then I stared too long, got caught, and he sucked his lip back in."

Jalen looked confused. "Wait a minute? Homie was pouting?"

"No. See, the left side of his upper lip was way bigger than his right. Almost like he'd been punched in the mouth but never recovered."

"Dang, that must've been one hard punch."

"No, no. I think he was born like that, but I don't know. I never talked to him about it or anything. And he did a really good job of keeping it sucked in so that it looked normal. He only let it relax when he thought no one was looking."

"Oh, okay," Jalen said, like he was getting the picture.

I gazed straight ahead at the waning light, thinking about how much I hated that Miles felt insecure about his lip. How it made me want to hold his face in my hands, take the left side of his upper lip into my mouth, and give it a gentle suck. I couldn't say all of that, so I said, "But after school, when he was behind his easel, his lip was always relaxed and free. I loved seeing him that way."

"When he was just being himself," Jalen said, blue light from the dashboard illuminating his face.

I paused for a moment to take it in. "Exactly," I said, and looked away. I needed to focus. "Anyway, after he caught me staring, I played it off by asking how his self-portrait was going. He said he was almost finished, so I got up and walked across the room to see. And he stood up to look at it with me."

"And then y'all looked into each other's eyes and—"

"Come on, Jalen. This isn't some kind of romance movie.

We were examining his work. You know, as artists. We'd given each other a lot of constructive criticism over the years."

"Oh," he said, like he was disappointed in my story.

"You're missing the point. He'd painted his lips completely symmetrical," I said, frustratingly waving my hands.

"Okay," Jalen replied, like it was no big deal.

"But his lips were nothing like that, and this was a self-portrait, so I asked him where his lip was."

"You *what?*" he said, turning toward me with wide eyes.

"I mean, the words slipped off my tongue quicker than my mind could stop them."

"And what did he say?"

"Well, he asked me what I meant," I answered, the excruciating question killing me all over again . . . the denial of himself.

"And what did you say?"

"I told him that I liked his lips the way they were."

"That's good."

"But then he kind of searched my face with suspicion, like he was waiting for the punch line of a joke."

Jalen took a left off the main road, his face dimmed in empathy.

"But I told him he didn't have to hide it. That I didn't

want him to hide his lip from me anymore." I went quiet as I thought about what happened next, feelings of embarrassment and shame pricking the blanket of anger I'd covered them with. "I don't even know why I'm telling you all of this." I wished I could press rewind and give him the version of the story I'd given Justine, Cara, and Dani after I'd found the envelope in my art bin, which omitted the almost-kiss altogether and focused on getting caught staring at him.

Jalen looked over at me, his patient expression making me feel like he was holding my hand.

"Then I stepped closer to him, like, inches from his face. I know it was bold, but I'd dreamed of kissing him for two years and never did anything about it. I was almost out of time."

"I get that."

"So, we stood there, for what felt like a century, while I waited for him to kiss me. But he never did. He kept his lip sucked in and turned toward the window. And I went back to my side of the room, packed up my stuff, and left."

"Damn."

"Tell me about it," I said, feeling surprisingly relieved to have finally shared the truth with someone.

"Sounds like there was just too much pressure on it," Jalen said, accelerating to get up the steep hill that led to our houses. "Like, maybe it was too much for him."

I stared at the glowing blue ring around the speedometer and said, "Yeah," liking the way Jalen framed the situation. "He wrote me a letter afterward. Maybe he explains some of it in there."

"Wait, you haven't opened it?"

"No, what's the point? It's a lost cause now," I said, wondering if Miles wrote about his regret, his foolishness. "Anyway, forget about me, what about you?"

He turned into his driveway, bright headlights beaming through the dark trees on either side, and pressed the gas again to get up the hill. "What about me?" he said, smiling bashfully.

"Don't even try it. After everything I told you, it's time for you to give up the goods on your girl situation."

He laughed and brought the truck to a stop at the top of the driveway. Put it in park. Took his seat belt off but didn't get out.

I took mine off, too, and we turned to face each other on the worn leather bench seat, darkness around us like a cocoon.

"Well, I had this girlfriend pretty much all of last year," he began. "Nicole. She was new. Had moved here from San Antonio with her sister, who was a year older. I mean, everybody wanted to date them. You know how it goes. They were already beautiful, but their newness added that extra sheen."

I thought about asking to see a picture, so that I could see what he considered beautiful and compare myself to it. But I didn't want to hold the story up, so I replied, "Yeah."

"I wasn't really trippin' over them like that. I mean, Nicole was cool. She was in my French class, so I saw her regularly. We talked sometimes, you know, like people do. But then one day, I saw my name scribbled in the left-hand margin of her notebook."

"You sat next to her?"

"No, she sat three seats ahead. But that day, I was late and peeped it when I was walking down the aisle past her desk."

"Oh, she wanted you to see that."

"I don't know. Maybe. But from then on, it was gravy. I think we became boyfriend-girlfriend, like, the next day and were pretty much always together. That is, until she got the lay of the land, realized I wasn't cool enough, and went to the prom with this football player named Stan."

"That sucks. But your story was way too short. You can't skip over that much."

Jalen looked straight at me and asked, "Well, what else do you want to know?"

If there had ever been a time like that with him, I couldn't remember it. Us talking about relationships. Getting deep. In the hazy, blue-gray of the truck's cabin, it felt like we were in our own private world, where it was safe to talk about anything.

"Did you love her?" I asked, because it felt like the deepest thing I could think of.

His face got serious, and he answered, "No." Then he looked down and started pulling at the silk floral scrunchie I had around my wrist.

My eyes traveled down to his fingers, touching me but not. He seemed to be aware of it, too, because he wouldn't look up. Everything inside me swirled and swelled until I felt like I was about to burst. I peeked up. He caught my eyes, and we raised our heads together, staring at each other in silence—

A bang on the back of the truck, then Lena at my window yelling, "You comin' or what?"

It almost hurt to turn my head away from Jalen to look at her.

She didn't even try to hide the stank face she was giving us, but I rolled down my window anyway.

"Not tonight. We—"

"Don't worry about it," she said and walked off.

"Well, somebody's mad," Jalen laughed, rolling his window down, too.

"I know, right," I replied, enjoying the luxury of not caring.

After that, we fell back into our normal rhythm of talking about everything and nothing, and I reached down for the bag of snacks that we'd stopped to get at the Buc-ee's by the church.

Breeze blowing through the trees around us, we shared some cheese puffs and sipped on lemonades. I practiced the no-backwash technique but had no idea if it worked. The cicadas and crickets were like a chorus of rattlesnakes in the woods, and we turned the radio up. Rapped along to Kendrick Lamar's "Humble" and agreed that we were lucky not to know anything about syrup sandwiches. That grilled cheese was as far as our broke-but-hungry mastery had to go.

Later, when I cranked the door open to get out of the

truck to go home, Jalen said, "I'm taking you sailing next Thursday. And I don't want to hear anything about it."

I smiled, said, "Yeah, yeah, yeah," and forgot all about asking what was up with Genesis.

Chapter 24

"You're in the no-go zone. You gotta get out of it," Jalen shouted from the front of the boat.

Wind angrily blowing in my face, I kept my balance with a wide stance and turned the gigantic steering wheel to the right. It was almost as high as my waist.

"Better, keep turning," he yelled, pulling on a rope connected to the mainsail.

Another spin of the wheel and the wind didn't feel as pissed. I took a deep breath in, trying to relax. Sailing was nothing like driving a sport boat. It was slower and there were a lot more things to pay attention to.

"You're a natural," Jalen told me.

"Stop lying."

He laughed. "It's all about your relationship with the wind. You'll learn."

"Whatever, it's about way more than that," I yelled back, thinking about how he'd been walking around the boat, pulling all types of ropes—raising this, lowering that, adjusting the tension here and there. I didn't understand what possessed him to want to do this for the rest of his life.

"But we're sailing now, aren't we," he said, cheesing, walking toward me.

"I guess," I replied, reluctantly smiling back.

"And it feels good, doesn't it?"

"Yes," I admitted. With Jalen standing beside me, I stared out at the crisp blue sky meeting the twinkling water, feeling a breeze curl over my sun-soaked shoulders, and began to understand.

He glanced at me, and we both looked back out at the water. We went quiet for a few minutes. Then he turned to me and said, "I hope you know you can tell me anything."

Sensing a question in his voice, I looked down at the steering wheel. It was same unspoken question that had been popping up in random conversations all week. *Did you or did you not steal Stevie's boat to go joyriding with my sister and that boy you think is cute?* It was my guilt, constantly harassing me.

Begging me to confess every morning before we ran down to the lake and every night on the back of his truck. But the water and sky were always so beautiful, and we were growing so close. I didn't want to ruin it, so, I finally replied, "I know."

More minutes of standing beside him in silence and then he told me, "My mom called last night," and I imagined the sky curving at its edges, wrapping us back in our cocoon.

I looked up at him. "When was the last time you talked to her?"

"I don't know. Maybe a month ago," he said.

A speedboat zoomed past us, creating large waves in its wake, rocking our boat, and knocking me off balance, away from the steering wheel. I'd forgotten to keep a wide stance.

"Whoa," Jalen said, grabbing my waist with one hand and the wheel with the other.

A million tingles up and down my side, and I reluctantly steadied myself and took the wheel back.

"I told her I had over half the money for *Honeypie*," he continued. "You know she's the one who named her, right?"

"No, I never knew that."

"I didn't tell you about it when we were kids?"

"Maybe, but I don't remember."

"Well, Stevie had gone into Maud's Café for her country-fried steak and eggs, like she still does every Friday," he said, leaving my side to sit on the bench in front of the cockpit.

His words made me think about what Daddy had told me happened the morning Jalen's mom left. How she pretended to go to work like normal but instead drove to Perry's Used Cars, sold her Chevy, and hopped on a bus to New York.

"But that Friday happened to be the day after Stevie had bought the boat," he continued. "Her first one with a cabin, so she was extra-excited, telling my mom all about it. But when my mom asked Stevie its name, she didn't have one. So, my mom suggested she call it *Honeypie*, which was her nickname for me," he said, smiling with boyish pride. "Anyway, Stevie liked it so much it stuck. And as a thank-you, she invited me and my mom to go sailing on it with her the next weekend. That was my first time ever sailing."

The wind changed directions and I turned the wheel slightly to the left. "So that's why you love sailing so much," I said, trying to sound as happy as he did.

"Well, that's definitely where it all began. I have my mom to thank for that."

"I guess." My voice was so bitter it surprised even me.

But I couldn't imagine wanting to thank her for anything.

"I'm not saying I'm cool with everything she's done, but I can at least give her credit for that," he said, defending his mom. "And for taking me back after she saw how much I loved it. Stevie let us sail *Honeypie* for free as long as we refilled the tank, and my mom took her up on that."

"Sorry, I didn't know," I said, remembering now the times Jalen disappeared in the late afternoons and I didn't have anyone to play with.

"She says she's thinking about moving back. That's what she called about."

Thinking? I berated his mom in my head. The inadequacy of the word infuriated me. *Either you're gonna move back or not. Which is it? How about you keep your mouth shut until you're sure. How about that?* But aloud, trying to sound excited for him, I said, "Really?"

"Yeah, she was talking about me only having two years of high school left and not wanting to miss out and stuff like that," he said, his voice trailing off.

His hope, singed with hurt, wailed in my heart, but I pulled myself together and said, "Yeah, you can't get back the time you lost. But it would be great if y'all could take advantage of the time you have left." Mom's words. I couldn't believe I'd just repeated them, but they were better than anything I had.

"Yeah, everyone deserves a second chance."

I stared at the blue lake, wondering if that was true. Wondering if I deserved a second chance, too. Again, I considered confessing right then and there but told myself it wouldn't be right to hijack the moment. That it would be better for both of us if I just never took Stevie's boat out again.

Feeling one door crack open and another shut, I adjusted the wheel to the wind, and we kept sailing. Beyond the beach we always down ran to, past the lighthouse and the tall hills standing behind it, around the bend and another ten miles to the north side of Alula Lake, out west by Cranes Park where I forced myself to stop thinking about the fisherman finding Gigi's body, and back to Stevie's.

When it was time to dock, Jalen took the wheel.

Standing beside him, a tiny fire swirled inside me as I wondered what the afternoon meant for us. He'd shared so much.

Backing into the slip with ease, he said, "Docking instruction is gonna have to come a little later for you. Maybe in lesson three."

Every good thing inside me swelled at the thought of spending more time with Jalen on the lake, and I said, "Whatever you think, Captain."

He looked at me and smiled with the brightness of the whole sky, and I felt more full of him than I'd ever been.

When he offered me his hand to get out of the boat, I took it. He helped me up, and I accidentally stepped on his foot. "Sorry," I said, looking into his eyes. *For everything. I'll do better, I promise. I'll start acting like I have some sense.*

"It's okay," he replied, and I swore he'd read my mind.

I think I love you, I told him but didn't dare say it aloud.

Time slowed as we stood on the dock . . . my right sneaker touching his left . . . our eyes sharing invisible messages . . . my lips itching for a kiss.

But neither one of us leaned in.

What She Missed

There was a fire whirling inside of him, too, and it was achingly hard to resist. But he remembered her tricks, her excuses, her bad moods, her distance.

They had given him a glimpse of what she was capable of and had reminded him that there was still so much to learn about her. She was hiding something, he knew. And he'd hoped the wind and water would help her open up. He waited and nudged and waited and shared and waited, staring into her eyes on the dock. But she wasn't ready to give it away. And he wasn't ready to get hurt by her.

Chapter 25

*S*hort hairs all over the bathroom sink and I had nowhere to put my makeup bag. I hated when Daddy used my bathroom to cut his hair and trim his beard. It was always after Mom had taken another one of her long hot showers and steamed up their mirror. He usually at least cleaned up after himself, but it's like he left in a rush—hair everywhere and clippers still on the counter.

Jalen had texted me thirty minutes earlier to say he was back, and I'd taken all that time just to choose an outfit—a cute magenta sundress with yellow flowers. Normally I went over there in whatever I was already wearing, but that night felt different. We were in a new space with unspoken feelings, swelling and stirring and making me feel like I was about to burst. That night, under the stars, surrounded by trees, we were bound to forget ourselves. And I needed to look good when it happened.

I stormed down the hall into the kitchen where my parents were slow dancing to a Stevie Wonder song playing on Daddy's phone on the counter. Mom's hair—a poufy, stringy hot mess—was all up in Daddy's face but he didn't seem to care. Neither one of them noticed me.

I cleared my throat. "Um, hello."

Daddy opened his eyes. "Hey," he said, and let go of Mom.

"Hi," said Mom, her faced flushed.

I briefly looked away from them down the hall, half wishing I'd dealt with the messy bathroom myself. Their love had a funny way of making me feel left out sometimes. I didn't think it was intentional on their part, but I was aware they needed each other in a way they didn't need me. Could make each other happy in ways I couldn't. Shared things I was not a part of.

I looked back at Daddy and said, "Your hair is all over my bathroom sink. I'm trying to get ready to go over to Jalen's."

"Sorry, my song came on and I forgot all about that. Let me get out of your way," he replied, heading out.

Mom took the opportunity to try to get up in my business.

"You and Jalen sure have been spending a lot of time together this summer."

My face started blooming and I opened the fridge to hide it. No one could know how I felt about Jalen until I knew for sure how he felt about me. "Yeah, we've been best friends since we were five," I said. In truth, I was afraid he still saw me that way. Afraid it was the reason he hadn't leaned in. All the assurances I'd made to myself that he was just taking things slow, like he always did, were dead by the time I grabbed the orange juice.

"Wow, that's what? Eleven years."

Fear turning into anger, I closed the refrigerator door and snapped, "Yeah, you should know. That's when you started sending me up here."

She squinted her eyes, like she was trying to figure out what had just happened.

I placed the orange juice on the counter but didn't bother to get a glass. "And he's basically the only person I know here because Daddy's always gone with his truck, and I have no other way of getting around." It wasn't even true. Daddy was always back by dinner, and I'd clearly met other people. But I couldn't miss the opportunity to make Mom feel guilty about something.

"Well, we never go anywhere. You can take the truck out tonight if you want."

"I just said I was going to Jalen's."

"Okay, Indigo," Mom said, sighing, her eyes pleading with me to stop trying to fight.

It's Ebony! I wanted to shout but didn't know why. I thought I'd buried that name, to make room for Indigo, the person I was becoming. But there I was, whirling with love and fear, pulling the name up from underneath the ground.

"I gotta go," I said, not wanting to think about any of it, escaping out of the front door without even putting on gloss.

No phone, either. I had to make my way to Jalen's in the dark. Rocks crunching beneath my feet, I gazed into the black trees, imagining the worst things that could get me—snakes, wild pigs, and bobcats.

But as soon as I entered the woods, the smell of wood and earth greeted me. A bird flapped its wings goodbye and took off toward the open sky. Walking along the worn path through the oaks, tall grasses and weeds stroked my calves. The cicadas and crickets sang me a song. The onion and garlic, still on my tongue from the chicken and rice Mom had cooked for dinner, made my mouth hum with love until I thought about it. *Of all nights to leave the house without brushing my teeth!* I screamed at myself before I heard the laughter.

I smiled at Jalen's silly butt. *Probably laughing at something on his phone,* I thought. Then I heard a squeaky and high-pitched giggle and froze.

I knew it, I told myself, amazed by how much it still hurt.

The world blurred and I stumbled blindly until my eyes caught the yellow porch light and traveled over to the two forms sitting in lawn chairs on the back of the truck. I quieted my steps and crouched down in the trees, trying to blink my tears away so that I could see the truth for myself.

Their heads came together and slowly moved apart, and a raging burst of flames ignited behind my eyes. I immediately took off running in the opposite direction. *"How could you?"* I cried inside, imagining the imprint of Jalen's lips on her lips—their softness, their fullness. *Their love?*

No! I screamed to myself, envisioning their lips burning up.

I ran faster and the flames shot higher and flung themselves into the crowns of the trees, killing all the birds and insects, anything singing. Faster and the flames spread through the darkness like a wildfire until the world around me blazed.

A twig on a low-hanging branch caught my sundress and I tripped and fell. On my knees, trembling in sadness and confusion, I actually thought about praying. But I was never any good at it. Gigi used to say that when you pray, you're not praying for a change from God. You're praying to change yourself.

But it always sounded like a riddle, and the memory of it only annoyed me. *I'm not the one who kissed someone else!* I thought, seeing red.

Chapter
26

Reversing down our long driveway, the night raged hot in my body. I floored the gas to get over the big hill. Flew past the fruit stand.

How could he? I asked the dark trees before forgetting to see them. Before forgetting to pay attention to the dotted yellow line in the center of the black road ahead. Forgetting to feel the leather steering wheel beneath my grip. To taste the garlic still on my tongue. Forgetting everything real.

Pulling up between two cars I didn't recognize, I wondered how I got there. I let out the breath I was holding hostage in my lungs and turned off the engine, hoping to escape into the dark waters again. Hoping to have the lake's velvety blackness wrap me in its wildness and make me forget. But when

I pushed open the truck's door, bass was thumping through the air.

I hopped out, ran to the top of the stairs, and saw a sea of people with red plastic cups dancing on the beach. Not what I'd planned on, and I scanned the crowd for Craig, hoping he'd at least be down to take me out on a Jet Ski. But there were too many bare-chested boys with locs. Good thing there weren't as many girls with buzz cuts, and I started toward Lena and Rebecca, who were twerking around the fire. I figured they would know where he was.

"Hey," I shouted when I finally made it to them.

Rebecca smiled and waved.

I waved back, and Lena turned around to face the dude who was dancing on her from behind without even acknowledging me. Staring at the flock of small black birds flying over the skin on her shoulder, I told myself the way she made me feel wasn't important.

A grab at my elbow, and I turned to find Craig—sun-kissed and shirtless.

He leaned in, locs tickling my left cheek. "Wanna get out of here?"

"Yeah."

He interlaced his fingers with mine and led me out of

the crowd toward the dock. "Where've you been?"

I shrugged, feeling myself heating up all over again.

"You know as soon as you stopped showing up, Lena got bored with the boat and started throwing parties again, right," he said.

"I doubt her getting bored had anything to do with me," I responded, feeling flattered.

"True. Lena is wild. To the point where I don't know if I can deal with her anymore. I mean, she seemed cool at first. But now I see she's on some ole' mad-at-the-world type stuff and I can't be around that type of energy. It always ends up pulling you into its madness."

I pushed away a vague sense that he was describing me, too, and said, "Yeah."

"I can't even tell you how happy I am that you're here."

I smiled, enjoying the pick-me-up of being wanted by someone. "Same, at least we can Jet Ski."

"Wait, you don't want to take the boat out?"

I stopped walking. "But the keys?"

"Oh, Lena made copies a long time ago. Sneaking in and out of Jalen's room got old."

The idea of extra keys to Stevie's floating around town made me sick to my stomach. "How many?" I asked, and let go of his hand. "Maybe we should stick to the Jet Skis."

"I'm pretty sure she only made one copy," he replied, pushing his locs out of his face. "What's the big deal? It'll be just like old times."

I didn't answer.

"Come on. You know you want to drive the boat just as much as I do," he said, and gave me a flirty grin that started with a tiny flash of tongue and ended with a small bite of his bottom lip.

He was cocky, spoiled, and didn't seem to have great morals, but at least he wasn't going around kissing annoyingly perfect girls on the back of his truck. Also, he was ridiculously cute with a banging body. I couldn't leave that out.

"Race ya!" I yelled and took off running along the shore and then down the dock. *If Jalen can kiss Genesis on the back of his truck, then I can have fun with Craig,* I thought, making my decision simple. Plus, I would've put money on them sharing a bag of cheese puffs after I ran off. At least five dollars on Jalen teaching her the backwash technique. And thinking about it made me want to get even.

But when I turned around, Craig was barely jogging in his Gucci slides.

"Why you gotta be so slow?" I yelled back at him.

Thinking I was playing, he laughed.

I rolled my eyes at him for ruining the fun and walked the rest of the way down the dock alone. When he finally made it, I told him I wanted to drive.

Craig's arms around my waist, and the safety lanyard around my wrist, I backed the Jet Ski up slowly.

"You remember how to—"

"I got this," I said, interrupting him. Then I turned toward the open water, twisted the throttle, and took off, water splashing my legs and wind pressing into my face. But I was still mad. Faster and I still felt the same. Faster and faster and after a few minutes, it became clear that speed wouldn't do the trick. Nor would the stars in the sky above or the shadowy trees at the edges of the lake.

When we got to Stevie's, I pulled into the empty slip between the sport boat we usually took out and *Honeypie*. "Should've named it *Playboy*," I said under my breath, wondering how many times Jalen had taken Genesis sailing. How many times they'd kissed in the cabin below.

Craig heard "playboy" and thought I was talking about him. "Why does everybody always say that?" he asked, letting go of my waist.

Confused, I slid the lanyard off my wrist and turned the engine off.

"It's funny because I'm not a playboy in the slightest," he said, standing up and stepping onto the dock. "Like at all. I keep a girlfriend and I've never cheated once."

I looked up at him, searching for the sort of deception I'd missed in Jalen—the unsuspecting kind, neatly packaged inside pretending to be a good guy. But Craig and his bare chest and his seductive smile weren't pretending to be good at all. "Is that right?" I asked, holding out my hand to him.

"Yeah," he said, and helped me up.

"Maybe it's your hair," I suggested.

"Nah, everybody has locs these days."

"Not sandy brown ones that blend with their skin."

"I can't help what color my hair grows," he said, pushing his locs out of his face again.

"Yeah, just like you can't help running your fingers through it all the time, either."

"Stop playing," he said, and smiled, showing his ridiculously perfect teeth.

"No, you stop. You know what you're doing."

"What am I doing?" he said, biting his bottom lip again.

"Come on. You know you're cute."

"Oh, you think I'm cute?" He put his hand on my waist.

Feeling the heat of his palm through my damp sundress, I replied, "Maybe a little bit." I was amazed at how the night had turned around. "But cute isn't the only thing, you know," I said, thinking of honesty, friendship, and trust. Jalen's bright smile flashed across my mind, making me tremble with hurt.

Craig stroked my cheek with his other hand. "Of course," he said in a soft voice. "There are a lot of sides to me. Just like I'm sure there are a lot of sides to you. Being beautiful can't be your only thing."

No boy had ever called me beautiful, and I couldn't help but blush.

"Lena told me you paint. I love that. But I want to know more. Ever since that first day I helped you off the boat, I've wanted to know you," he said, thumb rubbing my waist, eyes staring straight into me like I was his one and only. "And I don't feel this way about a lot of girls. Especially not right off the bat. But you . . . you do something to me."

The boy was good with his words and his hands—dangerous, I knew. But that didn't stop me from wanting to lean in and grab his lips with my lips. Tongue him down right beside *Honeypie*, hoping she'd somehow fill Jalen in.

But I couldn't risk having a nasty-tasting mouth and being rejected again. "Umm," I said, stalling, looking beyond him at the trailer, wondering if Stevie had gum. I remembered seeing chips on the rack in front of the counter and searched my memory for gum.

He turned to look at the trailer and then back to me, "See, that's the reason we haven't gotten to know each other better right there. We're always riding on a boat or a Jet Ski. We need to relax somewhere."

"I know," I said, glancing at *Honeypie,* flickering with the ultimate chance to get revenge. "That boat right there has a cute little cabin down below. Maybe we can chill in there."

"You're a genius," Craig said, and didn't waste any time hopping on the boat and trying the door. "It's locked."

"I can go get the keys."

"You sure you want to be the one breaking and entering?" Craig asked.

A rational person might've heard the legal jargon and woken up to the seriousness of the violation they were about to commit, but I wasn't interested in being rational. "Yeah," I said, thinking of fresh breath, wet kisses, and one-upping Jalen.

"You know which number this boat is?"

"Yeah, yeah," I answered like I knew all there was to know.

"All right then," Craig said, and tossed me the keys. "Don't turn on any lights. Get in and get out."

As I walked down the dock, I felt a force at my back, egging me on in the game I was playing, making every step I took toward the night ahead with Craig feel extra pleasurable.

But as I slipped the key in the door, I looked up and was momentarily startled by my reflection in the glass window. That girl looked hollow, dead, like a ghost. And she had this desperate look on her face, like she was begging me to go home. Begging me to let a good night's sleep and the morning light make the situation new. But I pushed ahead anyway, snatching the scrunchie out of my hair and pulling my twists down to cover my face before turning the key to get in.

Inside, my nervousness swelled, and I began to feel nauseous and hot. *Get in and get out,* I repeated to myself and hurried past the fishing poles along the back wall toward the cabinet of keys behind the counter. I grabbed number eight, the only key with a brass compass, and was about to head out when a wave of heat forced me to the ground.

Sweat beading on my forehead, I felt like I was about to

throw up. *What's wrong with you?* a voice inside me whined.

"Nothing! Get up!" I yelled at her.

I want to go home, she cried.

"So you can sit around thinking about Jalen and Genesis all night when Craig is right here? I don't think so."

But I don't love Craig.

"Do I have to remind you of what just happened on the back of Jalen's truck?"

But how could he kiss her when he loves me?

"Oh, so you still think he loves you, huh? How could you be so stupid?"

Curled on the floor in the dark, I was being pulled back and forth between two very different sides of myself until I spotted a small green container on the counter. I reached up, grabbed it, and leaned back against the wall. Flipped open the top and poured the gum straight into my mouth.

Only three pieces tumbled out and I shook the cup for more. Nothing, and I pressed my teeth into the candy-coated rectangles and felt cool explosions on my tongue. Soon my whole mouth was bursting with sweet, icy mint. Nausea in retreat, I got up and got out.

"What took you so long?" Craig asked as he helped me onto the boat.

"The cabinet was stuck," I lied, handing him the keys.

"Oh, a compass," he exclaimed, examining it like a new toy. He flipped it over and ran his fingers across the back. "Look, it's engraved. It says *Honeypie*."

I didn't want to look. I felt too guilty. But Gigi always said that guilt was useless when you're going to keep doing what you're doing anyway. "Must be its name," I said, looking at the dark hills on the other side of the lake, pretending not to know. "Let's go inside."

Craig opened the door for me and said, "Ladies first."

I climbed sideways down the steep stairs and sat on the bench in the back corner of the cabin. The miniature curtains were open and yellow light from the lampposts on the dock shone through three tiny windows.

Craig sat down beside me, smelling like funk, sun, and faded cologne.

"When did you get gum?" he asked, sniffing around my face.

I giggled and replied, "Inside."

"You get me some?"

"No, but I can share," I teased him.

He lowered his eyes to my lips and looked set to lean in, but I wasn't ready yet.

"You must play football," I said, staring at his smooth, hard chest.

"No, I row."

"Row?"

"Yeah, for the team at my school. Y'all don't have a rowing team?"

"We don't have any sports besides dance. I go to an art school. Well, I used to."

"Used to?"

I explained how I'd moved from Houston because my parents lost their jobs. How my friends and I were growing further and further apart. And when he listened without pity, I told him about the trouble I was having with my self-portrait.

He talked about how he lived in a nine-bedroom house overlooking Lake Travis, but his parents were almost never home. How once before he turned ten, he'd skateboarded off a small cliff and broken his leg just to make sure they'd be there for his birthday, but now enjoyed the freedom of being on his own.

It felt easy talking to someone I didn't know, who didn't know me. And after thirty or forty minutes, I felt like I was ready and put a hand on his leg.

He looked at it, then at me, and leaned in. Our lips met, our tongues touched, and my body surged with electricity. Buzzing, I rolled the gum into his mouth. He smiled and chewed it a few times before sliding it back into mine. With his hand around my waist and my fingers in his hair, our mouths and bodies found a thousand ways to press together.

Then he ran his hand over my breast, and I panicked as I considered what might be up next. Waiting around on Miles, I'd fallen behind in the land of making out. For me, everything beyond kissing was a new frontier. I stopped. Then I looked down and noticed how wet we were getting the cushion.

"Sorry," Craig said. "We can take it slow."

Guilt started to creep in, and I hated Jalen for it. *Oh, so you get to kiss Genesis, but I can't get your stupid cushions wet?* "No, it's fine," I said.

I leaned back in and tried to roll my tongue over Craig's tongue, but I began to feel nauseous and hot all over again. I didn't want to stop so I started taking in huge gulps of air between my licks and sucks.

My heavy breathing must've turned Craig on because he pulled my body even closer to his and kissed me harder.

Then my mouth started to taste sour, and I tried to push

past it by forcing my lips to move wilder, my breath to go deeper. But I was hot, then even hotter, and a storm of acid started swirling in my mouth until I felt like I was about to throw up. I ran up the stairs and hurled my chicken dinner all over the cockpit.

Craig ran up the stairs behind me. "Oh my God! Are you okay?"

I grabbed the huge steering wheel, wet with my sick, and leaned over it. "Can you believe Jalen wants to sail the world? It's the stupidest thing I've ever heard," I said, too exhausted to care.

"Actually, I have a cousin who sailed the world last year," Craig said, looking at me sideways.

"Well, good for him," I replied, mad because Jalen had won and I was undoubtedly lost.

"Wait, is this the boat that dude is trying to buy?" Craig asked, pushing his locs away from his face. "Lena told me about it and sounded just as cynical as you."

I stared at him, a wave of shame washing over me, and answered, "What do you care?"

"Bro, whatever this is, I'm not trying to be a part of it. You need to clean up the dude's boat so we can go."

I turned away from him to the cockpit. Thought about

going back inside and searching for some paper towels and disinfectant, maybe a mop. Pictured the steering wheel, dials, screen, and radio shiny and clean—vomit vanished, no sign of me or Craig ever being there.

But then I spotted a piece of chicken on the walkie-talkie and heard Jalen saying, *"Venez m'aider"* in his French accent. It burned me up beyond belief, his bright face with Genesis and his dreams. And I decided to let him see the mess. A glorious monument of what he did to me.

Chapter
27

*R*ed light behind my closed lids and I hoped that the previous night had been a bad dream, but the acid taste in my mouth told me it was real.

I opened my eyes. Sun poured in through my window, and I wondered how the world could be so bright when I felt so dead inside.

Nobody cares, I reminded myself.

Then I heard a voice saying, *But that's what friends are for.*

Part of me wanted to tell Jalen to shut up and leave me alone. But another part wanted to believe I hadn't lost my best friend. Believe that the sun's brightness could somehow right the wrong Jalen had committed with Genesis and lick my mess clean. But then I pictured their heads together on the back of his truck, imagined chunks of chicken and rice spewed all over *Honeypie,* and lost hope.

I closed my eyes again, trying to erase the night from my mind. A few minutes later, I heard rhythmic taps at my window. *He hasn't seen it yet,* I realized, and hurriedly tried to hatch a plan to somehow get to Stevie's and clean up my vomit before someone found it baking in the sun. That would at least take care of my half of our problem.

But Daddy and Mom were gone with the truck and wouldn't be back until 5:30. Since Mom had started teaching multiple dance classes a day, they'd developed this routine of Daddy dropping her at the gym before he went to the jobsite in the morning and picking her up on his way home.

There were no Lyfts or Ubers in Alula Lake.

Rebecca! I thought hopefully. But I didn't have her number. I didn't even have Lena's number.

"You know I can see you lying there, right?" Jalen's voice carried through the glass.

Still in the sundress from the night before, I rolled over onto my feet, slid open the window, and plopped back down on my bed.

"Dang, what happened to you?" he asked, his bright face dimming quickly in concern.

I guessed I looked as bad as I felt. "Nothing," I answered, shifting my gaze to the trees behind him. I couldn't look at his face. It made me want to scream, *I thought you were my friend!*

"Are you okay?" he asked.

The question made all the tears inside me try to rush out.

He slid his bucket hat off. "Are you sick?"

Centimeters from crying, I still couldn't speak.

"Did someone hurt you?" he asked, clutching the windowsill, hat crumpling underneath his palm.

You! I wanted to yell but finally answered, "No."

"You can tell me anything. You know that, right? I hope you know that."

I looked at him, thinking of us both coming clean.

"Come on, Eb-Indigo. Talk to me."

I stared into his dark, worried eyes, imagining the trees circling us, creating another cocoon. "Why—" I said but had to stop and clear my throat.

"Why?" he repeated, urging me to go on.

"Why didn't you just tell me?" I finally pushed out.

"Tell you what?"

"Look, you don't have to hide it anymore. I already know."

"You know what?" he asked, thick eyebrows scrunching toward each other.

I held his dark brown eyes, begging him to cut the crap. I was giving him a chance to finally admit to having a thing with Genesis. A chance to explain why he led me on. How he could be my friend and act so careless with my feelings. That he got confused by her shininess . . . that he was sorry and loved me not her. Then I could forgive him and confess to kissing Craig and throwing up on his boat. Maybe we could even laugh about it all before he drove me to the dock so I could clean it up. But none of that would happen if he refused to level with me first. "Are you actually serious right now?" I asked, disgusted.

He took his hands off the windowsill and took a step back. "What are you talking about?"

"You know exactly what I'm talking about, Jalen," I said, glaring at him.

"I really don't."

I couldn't believe how easy it was for him to look me in the eye and lie. "You know what, forget it. That's it. I can't do this anymore." I stood up to close the window.

"Wait!"

"No, I'm tired of waiting! I'm tired of you coming over

here every day pretending to . . . to—" I wanted to say *have feelings for me,* but the words felt too presumptuous, made me too vulnerable to another rejection. "To be my friend!"

He grabbed the window frame and plunged his head into my room. "What are you talking about? I *am* your friend!"

Annoyed, I backed away. "No, you *used* to be! Just go!"

"You're trippin', Indi—"

"Me?" I rushed back up to the window. "You're the one who wants to laugh and play with me every day, who wants to sit up in your truck and encourage me to spill my guts. For what? So you can go off and—" I couldn't even bring myself to say it. "I swear I hate you! I should've listened to Lena."

"Lena?"

"Yeah, you know, the sister you think you're better than."

"I don't think I'm better than anyone. She's going through stuff. I just didn't want to see you get caught up in her—"

"Don't act like you care about me!"

"What are you talking about? I do care about you, Indigo. You don't even understand how much. I . . . I—"

"Shut up!" I screamed, and shoved him.

He looked down at his chest, surprised, then back up at me.

Blazing with anger, I stared at him, trying to squash all feeling I had for the boy I'd known since I was five . . . who I'd swum with and raced a million times . . . who regularly lured me out of my misery to sit by the lake and under the stars . . . who I felt closer to than any friend back home.

I started to slide the window down and he pressed both hands to the glass to stop me. I pushed harder, and he tossed his hat through the gap before it closed. It landed on my right foot.

The hat was old and faded, but it had all the luster of the lake and sun . . . of Jalen. Annoyed by how much I yearned to pick it up and press it into my face, I kicked it across the room.

He stared at me like I was a stranger and I scowled back like, *You have some nerve.* And we stood there like that for what felt like hours. Still and quiet. His confusion against my fire—the only thing keeping my tears back. Until he walked off and the cold began to roll in. I welcomed it, the iciness. The way it numbed me and made me forget. Named it beautiful before pulling my curtains shut to block out the light.

What She Missed

Genesis was gay. The first time Indigo had met her, she'd peeped the multicolored scarf around her neck. The second time, the rainbow Vans. But busy feeling threatened, she never put the pride gear together.

There was no kiss. Jalen and Genesis had gotten close to look at the baby scorpion still crawling on the arm of his lawn chair. Minutes before Indigo saw them, Jalen had insisted Genesis snap his picture with it as part of her series of portraits called *People in the Dark*. She did, but only to give them something to laugh about while they waited. Genesis was way more interested in photographing his crush, neighbor, and childhood friend.

She was the perfect subject—moody, raw, and beautiful.

Afraid to approach her directly, Genesis had asked Jalen if it was okay for her to come over after he got off work. Promised to be quick. In Jalen's mind, it was a win-win. Help his friend and hopefully help the girl he'd always loved to better see herself.

Chapter
28

I didn't want to move. It felt too hard. Required too much. But my bladder wouldn't lie dead with me. Would not forget. Would not go numb.

On my way to pee, I caught a glimpse of myself in the bathroom mirror. My three-week-old twists had loose strands sticking out of them in all directions. The half-moons under my eyes were sunken and dark. My black bra straps were hanging out, and I was still in my sundress. It had a dried yellow vomit stain going down the center. *At least it matches the flowers*. I laughed.

I stared at my reflection, mesmerized by the fact that she didn't care. No more looking at me sideways. No more judgment. I bet I could even cut off my hair without her eyeing me funny. The clippers were right there in the corner of my bathroom sink. The cord wrapped neatly around them as if Daddy had left them just for me.

I picked them up. Plugged them in. Flicked a black switch on the side. They buzzed. They must've buzzed. But my hand didn't register the vibration.

I pressed the blade to my right temple.

Lena and Rebecca did it and it looks cool. Saweetie and back-in-the-day Solange did it, too. It's not a big deal.

And neither was the fact that I'd been growing my twists since my first summer at Gigi's house. Or that they were halfway down my back when it was almost impossible to get that kind of length with 4c hair. Or that I used to spend nine hours every other week untwisting, detangling, washing, conditioning, and retwisting them. Or that I loved them.

I couldn't remember what I loved. Or who or what loved me. I moved the clippers in a straight line from temple to neck. Forehead to neck. Again and Again. Chunky twists falling to the floor, puddling around my feet like a tiny black lake. I waded in it alone, gazing at my shaved head like it belonged to somebody else. Then I stepped out and went back to my dark, messy room to get into bed.

While the world kept spinning, I was swimming across

dry land trying to reach the sea. An ancient ship cruised by but wouldn't rescue me. *"Venez m'aider! Venez m'aider!"* I screamed until the ship was long gone. My limbs went limp, and I slid deeper into the earth's hot crust. Past mountains, birds, and blue skies, until a shark swam near and I stretched my jaws wide to rip it apart.

A knock at my door and I felt cold and wet. My dress. The sheets. Horrified, I rolled over to face the window, wishing I could go back to being a monster, drowning in dry land.

Mom came in and crawled into bed behind me. She had to feel the wetness, smell the sickly sweet, but she wrapped her arms around me. Kissed the back of my head—lips to scalp, no twists between—and an ache shot across my chest that I thought might break me.

I wailed.

"Oh, Ebony," she spoke my name, the one she'd given me. And it was like a portal back to being a child again, her child, counting nothing against her.

She held me for a long time. In silence. In stillness. And I wept, remembering her love. I'd questioned it for so many years and there it was, reminding me that I wasn't alone.

Then she began to peel her body away from mine and

panic swam through me. *No,* I yelled to myself, but she left the room anyway. I started to sink back into my dark hole when I heard the bath water running. Heard her humming the song she'd sung to me as a child. I tried to remember the lyrics but couldn't.

After a few minutes, she came back to me, pulled my covers off, grabbed my hand, and led me across the hall. The bathroom was dark with a small candle lit on the back of the toilet. It smelled like vanilla. I stared at its dancing flame while I undressed, remembering the fire in my eyes the night before.

Mom touched my shoulder and I jumped, naked and breathing hard. She helped me into the tub, and I lowered my body into the warm water, beads of oil floating around me, salt crystals poking me in the butt like tiny shells.

She gathered my clothes off the floor and whispered, "I'll be right back. Try to relax."

I nodded and she left.

I automatically reached up to tie my long twists into a knot, but of course, they weren't there. I'd lived with them for so many years that it was hard to believe they were gone. And it reminded me of how I'd felt when I'd learned that Gigi died.

I loved Gigi way more than my hair, I assured myself. I wrapped my arms around my knees and remembered how I hadn't gone to her funeral. While Daddy and Mom traveled to Alula Lake, I'd stayed behind at Justine's house because I didn't want to see Gigi lying dead in a coffin. I didn't even want to be in the same room. I had enough images haunting my mind as it was.

At Justine's we ordered veggie pizza and watched a funny movie. At first I felt bad for enjoying myself, but I kept eating and laughing anyway. Like I didn't love her. Like I wouldn't miss her. Like she wasn't a mother to me. Like the thought of never swimming with her in the lake again didn't make me feel sick.

I pressed my face to my wet legs and began rocking back and forth. "I love you. I love you. I love you," I repeated until Mom returned.

"You're okay, Ebony. You're okay," she said, helping me up. Then she dried me off, slipped a cotton nightgown over my head, and led me outside to the three wooden chairs on the front porch facing the setting sun.

Sitting with the light on my face and in my eyes, I imagined Gigi swimming in the lake down below, halfway to the lighthouse in her white swim cap. Flipping to her back when she tired. Floating with the warm sun on her face, silently inviting me to join her.

I started to stand up, but Mom, who was sitting beside me, grabbed my hand and held it softly.

"Do you want to talk about what happened?" she asked.

I stared at the trees, rattling with crickets and cicadas, and thought about Jalen. He'd be back from Stevie's soon but there would be no text. I wondered if he'd found my sick, if he was the one who had to clean it up. *No.* I shook my head.

The door creaked open, and she said, "Okay, we can talk later."

Daddy settled in the chair on the other side of me. He smelled like soap and was in a clean white tee and basketball shorts.

"I'm gonna get dinner started," Mom said. She squeezed my hand and left.

Daddy glanced at me and then at his phone. "How about some tunes?" he asked.

"Okay," I replied.

He started playing "My Girl" by the Temptations, and I thought about how I didn't have any sunshine. I already knew where this was going and there was no way he was about to get me to dance. He smiled at me, and I rolled my eyes like I wished he would go away even though I wanted him to stay.

For several minutes we sat still, the air thick with his worry, with my defensiveness, with his not knowing what to do or say. Then the monster in me dissolved and I laughed at his big toe poking through his white sock. It was something Mom and I always joked about because his big toes were disproportionally larger than the rest of his toes and wore holes in all his socks. But that evening, me and Daddy laughed extra hard.

Halfway into the Temptations album and a reluctant game of I Spy, Mom called us in for dinner. Mashed potatoes, broccoli, and broiled chicken. A few bites in, she cleared her throat and looked over at Daddy, a signal that they were about to team up.

"So can we talk about what happened now?" Mom asked.

My mind began to run off, away from the table to my old school and friends and dreams, past the studio with the blue blotches over my faces, through the woods, over to Jalen and Genesis, stumbling to the ground with fire blazing all around. Up and sprinting toward water, past Lena dissing me, onward, then making a wrong turn. Crimes and kisses and throw up simmering in the sun. Fighting with Jalen and the world going cold. Numb. My hair a lake on the floor. Dead. Gigi. I didn't even go to her funeral. The dreadful cloud stalking my future. It all clawed at me, and I ran faster, trying to get away, but it wouldn't let me—

"Indigo," Mom said urgently, using the name I'd most recently asked to be called.

Actually, I prefer Ebony I wanted to reply. *Something about the way you called me Ebony earlier made me feel like I was home.* But I'd switched back and forth so many times, I knew I'd sound like I'd lost my mind.

"We need to know what's going on with you. Please talk to us," she continued, her eyes pleading with me.

I looked down at my plate and pressed my fork into the potatoes. What she was asking felt impossible. Way too much to articulate.

"We can't help if we don't know," Daddy joined her, dropping a chicken bone, gristle gone and all, on the plate. He wiped his mouth with his napkin. "And don't worry about getting in trouble or anything like that. You can tell us anything, no matter how bad. Okay?"

"Anything," Mom reiterated. "Now, what happened? What made you cut off your hair?"

I don't like myself anymore, I almost said. But instead, I kept playing with my potatoes and answered with a shrug.

And the next morning, in my emergency Zoom therapy

session, when Ms. Kristi asked, "So what's been going on?" in her annoyingly lighthearted way, I shrugged again.

And the day after that, I kept shrugging.

But on day four of Mom and Daddy taking off work to hover over me, I finally blamed it all on teenage heartbreak. After taking a bite into the warm biscuit that Mom had made from Glamma Ella's recipe notebook, I told them I'd fallen in love with Jalen's friend Craig, but that he loved someone else.

They were surprised it wasn't Jalen himself but were relieved it was only boy drama.

Then Mom told me about her teenage love, Reggie, who ended up having another girlfriend at a different school. She'd found out when the girl joined the same ballet studio. Apparently, the girl wasn't cute and couldn't even do a basic pirouette, but her parents owned a diner and always hooked Reggie up with free sandwiches. Still, Mom had cried about him for two weeks and missed three days of school.

After breakfast Daddy evened out my hair, and I smiled and posed in the mirror like it wasn't so bad. When I walked into the living room, Mom jumped off the sofa and told me how beautiful I looked. I didn't believe her until she asked if it would be okay if she cut hers, too. She was tired of dealing with hair, and I was just the inspiration she needed.

More buzzing from the bathroom, and Mom walked into the living room and did a spin. Clutching a decorative pillow to my stomach, I forced myself to smile through the nausea I felt at how beautiful she looked. At how she made everything seem so easy.

By the late afternoon, they weren't paying as much attention to me. Mom practiced the Zumba routine she planned to do the next day, and Daddy was on his computer looking for his first lot to build on.

And when I sprinkled in some attitude about not having any orange juice to go with the tacos for dinner, they ate it up. Thought I was back to normal.

I judged them for being stupid and continued to keep my feelings to myself.

What
She
Missed

She was so close. Almost there. If only she would've been open. Honest. Maybe then she could've glimpsed herself. Made space in the hurt for her light.

Taken more responsibility for herself. Returned to loving and being loved.

Chapter 29

Lying on the sofa, still in the T-shirt I'd slept in the last three nights, I clicked on TikTok. Scrolled. Snapchat. Scrolled. Instagram. Scrolled. Apparently, Justine, Dani, and Cara were still doing their cleanse. *Good for them.* Instagram again. News Top Stories. It's an emergency! Hunger called me to the kitchen. Orange juice and turkey bacon. Still an emergency! Back to the living room. Tried to learn a few dances on TikTok. I was terrible. Kitchen again. Walnuts and raisins. Refreshed TikTok.

Kali, a girl in the vocal music program with Justine, danced in her bedroom in an oversized Houston's Academy of the Arts T-shirt that hid her shorts. Her movements were stiff, and she had this desperate, trying-to-be-sexy look on her face. But I still watched her video six times, jealous of her long black hair. Annoyed that she'd get to go back to school in a month and cry to Justine about the latest boy who was doing her wrong.

I wanted to call Justine and cry about everything. It would've been such a relief to get it all out. Instead, I made a grilled cheese sandwich and rinsed some grapes. Watched a few videos about assault in the digital world as I ate.

I was working hard not to think about Jalen or Gigi or my hair or how messed up I felt. But there was too much quiet in the house. Long stretches of time not broken up by pounding the dry earth with my sneakers or hiding from the sun or gazing at the sparkling blue lake or being annoyed by anyone.

At the kitchen table, staring at my plate of a few too-soft grapes, the quiet came after me. Insisting that I look. Listen. Understand.

Instead, I swiped Instagram off my screen and clicked on the blue icon with the white envelope. An email from Mr. Marshall with the heading "Self-portrait due August 15th." The words felt like an attack, and I put down my phone.

Through the window across the kitchen, I could see the studio out back. The reflection of sky, trees, and the fire pit in its glass doors. I hadn't opened them in almost two weeks. The girl with the blue blotches over her face was inside and I didn't want to see her.

What are you so scared of? a voice asked.

I grabbed my plate and stood up.

You can't avoid me forever.

I tried to ignore it, rolled the soggy grapes into the trash, and put my plate in the dishwasher.

I hate to be the one to break this to you, but—

I ran my hand over the short, prickly hairs on my head to shut up my brain and got a whiff of my underarm. *Dang, I'm musty.* I pressed my nose a little farther into my stench and took a deep breath in before pushing myself away from the sink and into the studio.

It was hot inside. I found the remote on the carved ebony pedestal and turned the air on. Even though it would take awhile to cool down, I stayed because all my work on the walls and tables seemed to know something I didn't know, something that hinted at hope.

But then I saw my last attempt at a self-portrait, still on the floor in front of the far window, squaring me up. I thought about retreating to the house, but figured I'd have to get past the girl with blue-black blotch over her face if I was ever going to complete the assignment. As much as I wanted to forget about it and not care, I didn't want to flunk Mr. Marshall's class.

I squeezed my hands into fists and walked toward the cardboard, trying not to think about all the times I'd failed before.

"You again," I said, standing over it.

Silence.

Already sweating, I started to get pissed. I couldn't believe that after almost a whole summer, this was all I had. The reality felt cruel.

I picked up the cardboard and ripped it in half. Quickly tore those pieces into four. Again and again, getting hotter and hotter, bits of thick, brown paper falling to the ground. I kept tearing them in two, wilder and more ferociously, like they might try to rise up and kill me if I didn't kill them first.

Whole studio feeling like a furnace, I got down on my knees and kept shredding, clawing at the bits without thinking, almost like I was in a trance. Until a bead of sweat rolled down my inner thigh and reminded me of the fact that I'd peed the bed. I snapped out of it, ashamed and frightened of myself. I ran out of the studio and got into the shower.

Eyes closed and hot water beating the back of my neck, I imagined floating on the lake, sun bright red behind my closed eyelids before I caught myself, scrubbed my armpits, and turned the water off. Grabbed the towel from the silver bar and wrapped it around my chest. Saw my reflection in the mirror and paused, amazed by how much I looked like Mom.

Pretending to be Mom, I shook my hips. Shimmied my chest. Did the move where she circles her hand around her head and steps to the side while simultaneously extending her arm. But I wasn't anywhere close to being as good as her. In any of the ways—moves, body, ease. I told myself I didn't want to be and dropped my towel to the floor, imagining myself as Lena instead.

I smiled darkly and then not at all. Looked my naked body up and down, envisioning tattoos in all the right places. Put a hand on my hip. Decided it was too sassy, not her style. Leaned my head slightly to the left and back. Still not right.

Looked myself straight in the eye and didn't like the way it felt. I turned the light off, put some clothes on, and found something to watch on Netflix until Mom and Daddy got back.

"Can you hand me that?" Mom asked, pointing to the canister of rolled oats on the counter beside me. She was still in her workout tank top, and her shoulders and arms looked stronger.

I passed her the oats, and she reached to put them on top of the fridge, pointing her right toes. She didn't ask me to get anything else, I guess because I was moving too slow.

So I leaned back on the counter, listening to Daddy singing in the shower and watching her gracefully move around the kitchen unpacking the groceries. She looked so bold and full of life, and I was envious that shaving my head hadn't done the same for me.

"What?" she asked, kneeling in front of the opened refrigerator drawer, holding a head of cabbage.

I stared at her face, still flushed from sweating all day, shining in the light of the fridge, and wondered if I was a disappointment to her. Wondered if birthing a child so physically similar but who was so messed up that she peed the bed at sixteen made her feel like a failure. "Nothing," I replied.

"What?' she asked again, not buying my answer.

"Nothing," I whined.

"I saw the email from Mr. Marshall today. Is that what's bothering you?"

I should've realized that he'd loop my parents into the

situation. He'd warned me that he would after I didn't reply to his last email, but her words still came as a shock.

"I thought you already handed in your self-portrait," she said, unpacking the last grocery bag. Wine, cheese, pepperoni, crackers, and chocolate—the ingredients for the Friday night pre-sex ritual my parents thought I was still too stupid to notice.

Gross, I thought, and said, "No, I decided to do something different. But it's not a big deal."

"Okay, how's the new one coming along, then?" she asked, as if the words coming out of my mouth were still trustworthy.

"It's almost there," I answered, in a hopeful voice, pretending to be in a better place. "I just have a few more details I want to add, but I should have it in way before the deadline."

"Good to hear. Can't wait to see it," she said and put the folded paper grocery bags under the sink to be reused.

"But going back to what's bothering me, I think I just need to get out of the house. Do you think I can take the truck tonight? Jalen's sister is having a small gathering at the beach."

She was already halfway to her bedroom, stripping off her tank top in preparation for another fifteen-minute shower.

The water had just stopped running, which meant Daddy was out. She briefly turned back to face me in her sports bra, flashing her shrinking waistline before unknowingly answering, "Yeah, it'll be good for you to get out and have some fun."

Chapter 30

"You did not!" Lena shrieked when I found her in the crowd. The beach party at The Cove was bigger than I'd ever seen it. Looked like the whole high school was there.

I smiled, happy to have her approval. I'd been afraid she'd either ignore me or have an attitude about me copying her, but she was way nicer than usual.

She rubbed my head aggressively, like I'd just scored a goal in a big game, and asked, "How does it feel to be free?"

I didn't understand what she meant, but said, "It's cool."

Rebecca, standing beside her, looked at me like I was unfortunate, and brought a joint to her lips. She took a pull, firing up the starry, orange tip, and blew smoke up at the sky. Then she handed the slender white roll to Lena, who took a puff before blowing smoke toward the back of a girl with silky brown hair who happened to be dancing next to her.

I hadn't smoked before, but I'd heard kids talk about getting high at school. Sometimes even smelled it in the third-story toilet near the instrument storage room, where I went if I couldn't hold in number two. I always inhaled deep when I detected the familiar smell but had never felt anything.

It was the same smell that used to come from Gigi's studio late at night. Same smell that used to hang in the air in the backyard whenever Daddy's brother visited before he got killed in Afghanistan. But Mom and Daddy had warned me on more than one occasion that it was bad for the teenage brain.

"Want?" Lena asked, offering me the joint.

I pinched the roll between my thumb and pointer finger, like I'd seen Lena and Rebecca do. *My brain is already broken, just like everything else in my life, so what do I have to lose,* I told myself before pressing my lips together over the roll. A little piece of weed got stuck to my upper lip, and I briefly pulled the joint away and tried to blow it off.

"You and all that gloss," Lena said and rolled her eyes.

I tried to get the tiny leaves off with my fingers, but my lips were extra slippery. I'd put on some gloss at the house and reapplied before I got out of the truck.

Rebecca eyed the joint, getting impatient. She was next in the rotation.

I brought it back to my lips and took a deep breath in. Fire scorched the back of my throat, and I started coughing.

Lena laughed, "Damn, girl. Take it easy."

I kept coughing.

"Has she even smoked before?" Rebecca asked Lena.

"Why you asking me?" Lena responded.

Still hacking, I handed the roll to Rebecca.

She took a drag.

I bent over, trying to get my lungs and throat to stop freaking out, but they wouldn't.

Rebecca grabbed my hand, like I was a little cousin who she was forced to babysit, and led me out of the crowd, along the shore, and back up to the folding table with the bags of chips, rows of water bottles, big cooler, and a stack of red plastic cups.

I grabbed a bottle of water and guzzled it, trying to calm my throat, until I was forced to come up for air.

Lena walked up and laughed. Which made Rebecca laugh, which made me laugh, which made us all laugh harder. And it made me think of Justine, Cara, and Dani. Of all the times we'd lost ourselves to silliness. "Oh my gosh. I love y'all so much," I said, trying to catch my breath.

"Love?" Lena laughed even louder, like it was the most ridiculous thing she'd ever heard. "Nah, you're just high, baby girl," she said, grabbing a plastic cup off the top of the stack.

"So high," Rebecca agreed.

Lena held the cup underneath the spout on the cooler, pressed the button, and a bright red liquid poured out.

"No, I'm not. I don't even feel anything," I said.

"Yeah, okay," Lena replied sarcastically and offered me the cup.

I drank the rest of my water and dropped the bottle into the garbage bag taped to the end of the table. Then I took a sip of the red concoction. It tasted like the cherry Kool-Aid we sometimes made over at Dani's house, and I gulped it down.

Rebecca grabbed the cup from me. "Yo, chill!"

"What?" I whined, noticing that my head felt light. That there was a soft layer over the starry sky, over Rebecca and the large crowd of people dancing and hanging around the fire behind her, over Lena, over . . . *Genesis?*

"Indigo! I've been looking for you," Genesis exclaimed before reaching for my hand.

I took it without even thinking. I knew I was supposed

to be mad at her, but I was still trying to catch up with myself. Everything felt at least three steps ahead.

Genesis smiled at Lena and Rebecca and said, "Hey. Sorry, y'all. Can I borrow her for a sec?" They both shrugged like, *Whatever,* and she pulled me away from them, down near the lake, as if she was trying to rescue me.

"You cut off your twists," she said, not offering a compliment.

"You brought a real camera to a party," I replied, staring at the professional-looking Canon hanging around her neck from a rainbow strap.

She laughed. "Yeah, I couldn't help it. How have you been?"

I rubbed my lips together and stared at her perfectly winged, neon-yellow eyeliner, trying to summon the words that would best express my hate for her. But all I could come up with was, "Is that really what you dragged me all the way over here for? To ask me how I've been?"

She looked flustered, maybe even a little frightened, but gathered herself and said, "Well, no. But I thought that would be a good place to start since I haven't seen you in a while."

"Oh, but I've seen you," I said, proud of my quick-witted response.

She squinted in confusion.

"Ask me where," I demanded, finally catching up to my anger.

"Where?" she replied, her voice swelling with unease.

"On the back of Jalen's truck. That's where," I said, slurring the last sentence.

"You saw us that night?" she asked, seemingly oblivious to the fact that I was drunk and high and mad enough to smash her in the head, to rub my palm in a thousand circles all over her precious baby hair.

"Why didn't you come over?" she continued. "We were waiting for you. Actually, that's the reason I pulled you aside tonight." She was emitting more and more of her usual shininess. It was like whatever she was talking about was literally giving her life.

Watching it was killing me.

"I wanted to ask if I could take your picture for this series that I'm doing called *People in the Dark*. I think you'd be—"

"Take it."

She looked confused.

"Take my picture."

"What, now?"

"Yeah, I don't have all day."

"No, that's okay," she said, and looked over her shoulder at a group of people playing Frisbee a little farther up by the dock. "I can catch you another time."

"If you want my picture, then take it now."

"Okay," she said apprehensively and removed the cap from her lens. Then she slid it in the back pocket of her lime-green shorts and pushed the power button. The lens extended and she brought the camera up to her face, looked through the viewfinder, and took a few steps back.

I figured that making her take my picture on the spot was ruining some elaborate plot she had against me. I had no idea what she was conspiring, but in the moment, I felt like I was ruining it. "Where is Jalen?" I asked casually, as a way of punctuating her loss, a way of saying, *Oh, you thought you could hurt me?*

Her face was still behind the camera, and she turned the lens a few times, this way then that, apparently trying to bring me into focus. "I don't know. I haven't talked to him in a while."

"What do you mean you haven't talked to him?" I asked, sounding way more bothered than I wanted to.

She stayed cool. "I think he's been busy at Stevie's or something. I don't know, but he hasn't been around. Haven't you talked to him?"

I stared at her, the night air rippling with my anger. Her indifference was making a fool of me. Of everything I felt for Jalen. Of everything I'd hoped for. "Nope," I said, doing my best to pretend like I didn't care about him, either.

"Really?" she asked, sounding surprised. "I thought y'all hung out all the time."

You can't be serious? I wanted to yell. But I wasn't about to have it out with her like I'd had it out with Jalen. I wasn't about to give her that win.

"There," she said to herself before she snapped.

A bright light flashed, making me squint.

"Yeah, sorry. I have to use the flash out here. The moonlight isn't enough."

Done with words, I stared straight into the camera.

"Okay," she said, like I was doing something right, and started snapping again.

I kept staring at her, harder than before.

She squatted down, elbows resting on her knees, and continued to shoot.

The photo session began with my anger toward Genesis but got darker and more personal from there. Each shot bluer and blacker than the next. I fought back, my poses like angry punches. But the night kept hurling its blood-curdling words at me, *Look at yourself. You're a mess. Open your eyes. You're the one doing this.* Riddles I ignored as I kept my eyes fixed on the camera, not smiling or pretending to be anyone else.

She stood up and brought the lens closer. Even closer.

It was more than I could handle, and I retreated too fast, tripped, and fell backward into the lake. Sharp rocks poking me in the butt and water drowning my ripped jean shorts, I began to cry. *Why?* I asked the silvery moon and stars. *Why does life have to be so hard?*

Genesis came rushing over to help me up and I yelled, "Just take my picture, okay!"

She backed up, tentatively.

"Would you hurry up, already!"

She slowly brought the camera back up to her face.

Staring into the dark lens, I felt alone and knew that I would feel like that forever. Knew that I would never become a painter. Never make any new friends. Never find anyone or anything to love again. I looked at the dark water, wanting to lie down in it. Imagined floating up next to a fisherman's boat in the light of the morning, dead.

A bright flash.

I looked up, saw people dancing, heard Too Short's lyrics blasting, smelled the bonfire in the air, and remembered where

I was. I got back on my feet and stumbled off toward the party, like nothing had happened, like Genesis wasn't even there.

"Wait," she yelled.

I turned around.

She walked up to me but didn't say anything.

"What?" I asked, annoyed, water dripping down my legs.

"You need a ride somewhere? Maybe to get a change of clothes?"

"They'll dry."

"Okay. Well, do you wanna play Frisbee? Me and a couple of friends started a game." She looked toward a small group of people near the dock, throwing a yellow disc around a wide circle.

I was good at Frisbee. Years of throwing a football with Daddy when I was younger gave me an advantage in most throwing games. I imagined feeling like a winner and replied, "Why would I want to do that?"

"Well, we'll be over here if you change your mind."

I turned away, searching the crowd for Lena and Rebecca. I spotted them dancing around the fire with a girl between them wearing white tube socks and a high brown ponytail. She was unusually thick and knew how to move her body.

I made my way through the crowd to them. It was hot so close to the fire, and I wondered why they didn't move back.

"Heeey," Lena sang at my return and waved her hands in the air.

I tried to mimic her and felt awkward.

High Ponytail started to spank Lena's booty to the beat of a rap song I'd never heard. Lena smiled, turned around, and High Ponytail passed her the joint. Then Lena took a hit and gave it to me.

The white roll had gotten way shorter, harder to pinch, and when I tried to smoke it, it burned my lips. I yelped and jerked my head back.

"Here, give it to me," Lena yelled over the music, reaching for it. "When I blow out, you inhale and then hold it in."

I nodded.

Lena took a long pull then leaned in so close to my lips that I was afraid she might kiss me and I wouldn't know how to react.

A cloud of smoke came toward my face, and I closed my eyes to take it in.

"Yaaas," a voice said. It wasn't Rebecca's, so I assumed it was High Ponytail's.

Lena kept blowing and I kept inhaling until I couldn't

anymore. Then I held the smoke in my chest. It burned and I wanted more than anything to let it out and take a deep breath, but I kept holding it until I felt my head go light again. When I opened my eyes and saw Lena's proud expression, the pain felt worth it.

"Whooa!" Lena said. She threw her hands up and started dancing.

I joined her. High Ponytail, too. Rebecca was already dancing with some dude in a baseball cap. He didn't have much rhythm, and she held his hands to help guide his movements. It was cute.

Staring into the fire, I kept dancing, moving my body in all directions without thinking. Slower or faster than the music, I didn't care. Sweat beading on the crown of my head and dripping down my temples without wiping it. Wet jean shorts rising farther into my crotch without pulling them down. Wild. Everything stirring and heating up under the stars, close to the fire. Forgetting myself.

Until a dude started dancing on me from behind. I looked over at Lena and High Ponytail, and they each had a dude grinding on them from behind, too. They started twerking, seemingly enjoying the new attention.

"Heeey," Lena said, cheering on High Ponytail.

"You betta work!" High Ponytail reciprocated.

I'd tried twerking a few times at the slumber parties we used to have at Justine's house. Dani was the only one who could get her booty to move like the girls in the TikTok videos. Justine was decent, but Cara and I were hopeless. Watching Lena and High Ponytail, though, I started to feel left out. So I arched my back and shook my butt any direction it agreed to go.

The dude behind me was the only one who noticed. "Yeah," he grunted, and I looked back. He wasn't cute.

He started caressing my waist.

It didn't feel good.

But I went along, ignoring my unease. I kept dancing, even though I was getting too hot, my mouth was parched, and I desperately needed some water. I kept going, ignoring the fact that my jean shorts were all the way up my butt and the rock or shell in my right sneaker dug into my heel with every step. I kept going along, not listening to the whispers that I'd already gotten hot enough, high enough, and wild enough. That it was time to call it a night.

Lena and High Ponytail took off their crop tops and shorts and threw them into the fire. It burned higher and the crowd cheered. All the commotion made Rebecca briefly stop dancing with Baseball Cap and turn around. She looked at Lena and High Ponytail, topless in their panties, like it was nothing new and went back to teaching Baseball Cap how to dance.

More and more people started watching Lena and High Ponytail as they bent all the way over—hands on the ground, butts in the air.

By the way the dude behind me started curling his fingers around the bottom of my tank top, I could tell he wanted me to join in.

I went along. Not taking off my shirt but my shorts. I figured they were wet and uncomfortable anyway. And I didn't throw them in the fire; they were too cute for that. Instead, I kicked them off to the side, then proceeded to shake my butt the best I knew how.

"Get it, Indigo!" Lena yelled. Then she and High Ponytail got up and started cheering me on. "Go, Indigo! Go, Indigo!"

The crowd joined in, and the chant grew louder.

I felt so alone.

"Go, Indigo! Go Indigo!"

It started to sound less like encouragement and more like a command.

"Go, Indigo! Go, Indigo!"

I forgot how to say, *I don't want to do this. I'm not comfortable with showing my body to this many people. Stop touching me. I don't like it.*

I looked at Lena, hoping she would remind me of how to stop, but her eyes were aglow with a mixture of danger and carelessness.

"Go, Indigo! Go, Indigo!"

So I kept going along, feeling more and more alone amidst the crowd's cheers. I went along and along until I felt myself split into two. One side getting gnawed by the crowd and the heat, and the other side looking out at the lake, beyond the fire. I imagined myself swimming in the cool water. Imagined flipping onto my back and letting the water hold me. Until I spotted a Jet Ski in the distance and remembered the night on *Honeypie* with Craig.

"Go, Indigo! Go, Indigo!"

Shame started clawing at me and I turned my attention away from the water and back toward the fire. But there was a monster in the flames. She hissed and growled and yelled at me. *Look at yourself! You're a mess! Open your eyes! You're the one doing this!* But I was too hot and scared to listen. She lunged at me, her orange arm spiraling toward my face, and I covered it with a blue blotch.

"Go, Indigo! Go, Indigo!"

I felt nothing. I kept going along. As I put my hands on the ground and my butt in the air, I spotted Genesis coming around from the other side of the fire. She was holding hands with a girl who had short blond hair. Then Jalen came around the flames, and I began to feel things again.

See things.

Like Genesis and Jalen really weren't like that. Suddenly it became so clear. Their heads coming together and moving apart, like friends sharing a moment. No bodies pressing together. No lips. *How did I get it so wrong?*

"Go, Indigo! Go, Indigo!"

It was enough to remind me of how to stop. But I didn't.

"Go, Indigo! Go, Indigo!"

I pressed through the humiliation so that I wouldn't look humiliated. I knew I would have to walk past most of these people in the halls when I went to school in the fall. And I'd rather be the wild girl than the girl everyone felt sorry and embarrassed for.

"Go, Indigo! Go, Indigo!"

So I sank my hands into the tiny rocks and shells. Shook my butt in the air.

"Go, Indigo! Go, Indigo!"

The fire got hotter and hotter. Hungry for the back of my head, neck, and shoulders. Consuming me.

Two hands around my waist, pulling me away from the fire, and I turned around and saw Jalen.

"What the hell is wrong with you?" he yelled.

I didn't have an answer.

I grabbed my shorts and ran away from him and the humiliation and the regret, away from the fire, fumbling and squeezing my way through the crowd, like I was being hunted. And when the party thinned out, I sprinted across the rest of the beach, up the stairs, and to the truck I'd left unlocked. Grabbed the keys from the cup holder, started the engine, and sped off.

Chapter 31

*T*he road and the trees and the sky had all disappeared. Everything around me was engulfed in flames, whirling, and I struggled to piece together where I was.

A memory jumped out of the fire of me riding a pink bike with training wheels. Mom's voice yelling, "Slow down!" before I flew around a corner, tipped over into the grass, and started wailing with my fists balled up.

I wanted to lean in and tell my little self that everything would be okay, but she spun around and vanished back into the blaze.

Another scene emerged. I was at our old kitchen table and my hair was in four braided ponytails. I wanted bacon, not oatmeal. Orange juice not apple, and I whacked my favorite mug. Watched Princess Tiana fall to the tile floor and shatter.

Again, I wanted to tell myself to calm down. It wasn't that serious.

A watercolor of a windmill against the sunset with a white ribbon hanging from it. Holding the painting, I glared at the camera after winning third place in the Houston Livestock and Rodeo Art Competition in the fourth grade.

I never submitted artwork to the contest again, even though I was good enough to win. Even though all submissions were eligible for the auction, where pieces have been sold for two hundred and fifty grand.

In the distance I heard a moan, deep and painful. I covered my ears. Sweat ran down my forearms and dripped from my elbows, and I desperately looked for a door, a path, any way out of the fire.

My younger self in the lake with Gigi, too scared to put my head under the water. Jalen kept going under to show me it was okay, but I only got mad. I waded to the shore and ran back to the house through the woods, alone and miserable.

I tasted blood.

The pieces of my life flew at me faster. Incomplete and out of order, but after a while I saw a pattern. Getting pissed and suffering, running away and suffering, over and over again on a loop. Whenever I was afraid or things weren't going my way.

The pattern was so clear, and then I couldn't see it anymore in the whirlwind of everyday things. Wildflowers, snake holes, a marker, a ladder, Daddy's silver belt buckle with the longhorn, three mosquito bites on my arm, thunderstorms, my alarm clock, the sky, a black tufted bench with silver legs, a wide-tooth comb.

I saw a beast with no face coming toward me, her limbs sculpted by flames. I tried to take off running, but my legs felt like they were buried in cement.

I was in the center of the fire, trapped, and she was getting closer. Getting ready to claw me into a million pieces, I was sure of it. Probably even eat me.

I started screaming and cursing, trying to keep the beast away. But this only made her growl louder, her fire grow higher, and she started sprinting toward me.

Bracing for her to snatch out my throat, I saw my own face. It felt like a curtain lifting, and I remembered the words I kept hearing earlier that night: *Look at yourself. You're a mess. Open your eyes. You're the one doing this.*

Devastated, I stopped struggling and tried to make peace.

I love you, Mom. I love you, Daddy. So, so much. Thank you for everything you've done for me. This is not your fault. I love you,

Gigi. I love you, too, Jalen. You're my best friend. You always have been. Sorry I didn't listen. I love you, Justine. I wish I would've talked to you. And you, Cara. And you, Dani. I love everyone and everything. I love you, world. You're so beautiful. Even in the madness. And life. My precious, life, I wish I would've owned up to you while I still had the chance.

What She Missed

The long road ahead.

Chapter 32

I don't know where I am or how long I've been away. Minutes, hours, weeks? I try to open my eyes, but they're too heavy.

I allow myself to drift off again, this time to the woods, where I see a flower that I once knew the name of. I stare at the clusters of small, purple blooms until it comes back to me. *Heliotrope*, I remember gladly.

Then I hear a low, deep moan. Taste a mixture of metal and strawberry gloss. Feel the blood running from my nose . . . the ache along the back of my neck and under the seat belt strapped across my chest . . . the pounding in my head. Smell smoke. Sense the road ahead rushing back.

I hear the moan again, and my mind struggles to accept that I've hit something or someone. I don't want to open my eyes to see what I've done. Panicked, I imagine running into the dark woods and never coming back. Never seeing anybody I love again. *You can do it!* I try to convince myself.

But my longing to escape seems too familiar, and I get the feeling that it will only make things worse. I dare to open my eyes. A deflated white bag hangs out of the steering wheel. I slowly lift my head to the cracked windshield, smeared with blood, and my heart starts banging in my throat.

Another moan, the most awful sound I've ever heard, and I get out of the truck. The headlights shine on a wounded doe in the middle of the road. A sense of urgency overtakes me, and I climb back into the truck to call Jalen for help.

I don't know how long I sit beside the doe on the dark road. Staring into its wild eyes, listening to its cries, the trees and sky and headlights all fade away until there is only me and my burning shame. I let it consume me and wail with the deer.

"Are you okay? Are you hurt?" Jalen yells, running toward us. I can see now, with the addition of Jalen's bright headlights, that the doe's ribs are caved in. That blood is spilling from her mouth.

"I'm fine. It's just her," I say. I wipe my nose with the backside of my hand, but the dried blood doesn't go anywhere.

"You don't look fine."

"I am. I promise. Please, just help her."

"Okay, back up."

I stand to get out of his way and she lets out a low, deep moan.

"Shh," he says, kneeling beside her.

She moans again.

"You're okay," he tells her, and strokes the furry part of her head above her eyes. Her ears relax. Then he raises his fist and gives her a sharp blow below the head.

The crack of her neck breaking makes me flinch.

Still on his knees, Jalen places a hand on the doe's neck and closes his eyes, as if saying something privately to her.

When he stands up, I say, "I'm sorry."

He ignores me, grabs the deer by all four legs, and drags her to the side of the road.

"I hate that you had to do that."

"I'll drive you home," he responds coolly and begins to walk toward his truck. "You need to get your dad's truck over to the side of the road."

I wish he'd slow down so that I could give him a proper apology. I turn toward him, trying to come up with the right words, but I only get out another "I'm sorry, Jalen."

"Make sure to turn the hazards on."

I start crying again. I know I don't deserve to hear, *It's okay* or *I forgive you*. After everything I've done, that would be some God-level mercy and he's only a boy. But he doesn't know anything about what I experienced tonight. He doesn't know about the fire. How it gave me more clarity than I've had in all my sixteen years on earth. I'm a different person now, and I want him to know.

"Come on, Indigo. We need to go!" he yells like a parent urging a child to keep up. He's on the step of his truck with his arm hanging over the door.

I imagine how useless I must look to him in the bright light, just standing in the road crying, not doing anything to help, and I head to my dad's truck.

Behind the wheel, my guilt mixes with the blood on the cracked windshield and I begin to cry. Feeling sorry for myself, I cry harder, snot and blood running over my lip. *Nasty*, and I wipe it with the back of my hand before I put the truck in reverse and get it to the side of the road. Focusing on the small task rewards me and I quit crying.

"How much did you drink?" Jalen asks when I climb into his truck.

I want to tell him that I don't feel drunk anymore, that

fire and regret sobered me up, but I say, "I only had a cup."

"Wait, you've been smoking, too?"

I must reek of it, I think, and exhale hard but can't smell anything. "Like two hits, but really one unless you want to count Lena blowing—"

"Oh, I see. Since you only drank and smoked a little, you figured it was okay to drive. Have you lost your mind? You could've killed someone! You could've killed yourself!"

Killed . . . killed . . . killed . . . the word reverberates down a dark hole in my body, and I close my eyes and follow it. But it's cramped and depressing in there, and I want out. I open my heavy lids. "You know, for a second tonight, I thought I was going to die. There was this monster . . . and she was me, but I couldn't stop her."

He looks at me, half confused, half exhausted.

"It's crazy because I hadn't prayed in so long. But I think that's what saved me. I even prayed to you. Not that you could hear me. No one could, but it didn't matter because I could hear."

He dismissively shakes his head before turning away from me and starting the engine.

"I know you think this is the weed and alcohol talking, but it's not."

"Hmph."

"I mean, I may still feel a little slow or something, but I'm not out of my mind," I defend myself. "I'm trying to talk to you, Jalen. I know I messed up . . . I've been messing up. And I'm sorry. I wish I could go back and do so many things differently."

He puts the truck in drive, his eyes still straight ahead.

"Look, you don't understand, okay. I was keeping so much locked inside me that it literally tried to kill me to get out. Nobody was safe."

He drives a little farther up the gravel road in the wrong direction, past the deer, and then does a three-point turn to get us heading the right way.

"I'm sorry," I repeat, mostly because I'm starting to get the feeling that he's done with me and that he has every right to be. Putting on my seat belt, I stare at his face, shining with sweaty disappointment in the blue light of the dashboard, and say, "I almost wish you'd kissed Genesis."

He whips his head toward me in annoyance. "What?"

I try to meet his eyes, but they're back on the road.

"I thought I saw you kissing her on your truck," I tell him. "I know you didn't, but I'm just saying that if you did, there'd probably be more of a chance of you forgiving me right now."

Looking straight ahead, he squints in confused disgust.

"Maybe there was a part of me that wanted to think it was true even when I knew it wasn't," I considered, the words pouring from my mouth without a filter. "Maybe deep down I thought if you'd been kissing her behind my back, then that would somehow balance things out."

After taking a right at the corner, past a strip center under construction, he turns up the AC. When he pulls his hand away from the knob, I notice my silk floral scrunchie in the cup holder.

I don't want to get ahead of myself, I really don't. But I can't help but feel the edges of hope. I can't help but think that him keeping a piece of me from the night we spent hours talking is some kind of proof that we can come back from this. Tenderness fills me as I remember him pulling at the folds in the silk, his fingers almost touching me but not.

Jalen sees me eyeing the scrunchie and says, "You left it inside of Stevie's."

A flash of the silky band lying on the tile floor behind the cash register, then another one of chunks of chicken all over *Honeypie*, and my hope is gone. "I'm sorry," I repeat, hating how the words feel smaller and smaller each time they leave my mouth.

"Don't worry. I didn't tell Stevie it was yours."

"I'm not worried about that."

He whips his head toward me again. "You should be. I had to convince her not to call the cops!"

I stare back at him, wishing he could magically see inside of me, lay eyes on everything that's changed. "No, I meant I'm worried about you . . . us."

He quickly turns back to the road.

"I just don't want you to be done with me and everything we had to be, like, poof!" I say, making an exploding motion with my hands.

He ignores me.

"I should've found a way to talk to you sooner, I know, I should've. But I didn't want you treating me like Justine and them, like I was some kind of sad case. I wasn't a sad case!" I yell. And then hearing myself, I quietly admit, "Okay, maybe I was."

More silence.

"I cried for, like, a month after I found out we were moving, you know. My parents got me this therapist, but then I convinced them I was all better and started nursing my swollen eyes with these washcloths I kept hidden in the freezer."

He glances at me.

"I couldn't forget her anymore," I begin to cry. "I didn't want to remember, but I hated that I'd forgotten so much . . . so much of me was from Gigi. And nobody understood. They all had stupid moving checklists and cute outfits to shop for. And I had a home and school to kiss goodbye. I wanted to stay. I wanted to stay so bad, but it didn't matter. Ugh, and the stupid self-portrait."

He takes his eyes off the road to look over at me again.

A mass of words gathers in my throat, and I keep pushing them out, talking through my tears. "It was all so . . . exhausting. I was tired of feeling. I didn't want to care anymore."

He looks at me, his face soft.

"Who knew it would be so hard? And you and all your brightness surely didn't help," I say, managing a small laugh. I wipe my snot.

He almost smiles.

"You," I say and look at him in a way I've never allowed myself to before, with the deep ache I feel in my heart. "I didn't know if you were real . . . if we were real. I didn't know."

His eyes search me.

"I should've told you before. Then I would've known either way and wouldn't have started making stuff up."

His face stiffens as if he's waiting for more words.

"You know what I'm trying to say."

He doesn't respond, but I know he knows.

"Are you really gonna make me say it?"

"Say what?" he says slyly, and I can almost taste his knowing.

"I have feelings for you, Jalen. There."

He looks at me and, just like that, we are not the same as we were before.

"I realized it that night in your truck. Well, maybe before that. Definitely before that. Actually, it was probably the day we went up the hill and saw that boulder we painted as kids."

I shake my head to try to get back on track.

"Anyway, I wanted you to touch me, inside your truck, when you were pulling my scrunchie. It was like . . . oh my God . . . you don't even know. And every night after, I wanted you to kiss me, but you never did. And when you took me sailing, I was sure you would, but you still didn't. So when I saw you kissing Genesis on the back of your truck—"

"We were actually waiting on you."

"I know that now. I told you I was making stuff up. Anyway, things got real bad from there," I continued, trying to get it all out. "I mean, look at my hair," I said, running my right hand over my prickly head.

He looks at me, reaches for my other snotty, bloody hand, and holds it.

Heart racing, I stare at him, feeling almost grateful for the hell I just went through that led us here. Then I remember the missing pieces of my story.

"There should be some gum underneath your scrunchie," he says, going up the hill to our houses.

"Oh, you trying to tell me my breath stinks," I joke.

"Yeah, like weed and alcohol."

"Dang, I almost forgot about that," I say, feeling guilty about hiding the truth from my parents. *But so much of what I've done feels like it was done by somebody else,* I convince myself. *A girl who was me but who isn't me anymore.*

Jalen starts up my driveway, and I let go of his hand, wrap the scrunchie around my wrist, and dig in the cup holder for gum.

He comes to a stop and puts the truck into park. "You might as well let me keep it. It's not like you need it anymore," he says, and pinches at the silk folds in the scrunchie.

I take it off, he slips it around his wrist, and my heart is ten thousand tongues trying to find a way to tell him all the things I left out.

It would be easier if I didn't tell him, a voice says, using the same logic I just used for my parents. I take off my seat belt and turn to face him.

He does the same and says, "I can do the talking if you want me to. After they see your nose and all the blood on your shirt, they'll probably just be worried about you being okay. But you have to promise that you'll never drink and drive again."

"Never," I say, and mean it.

"Good. I'm sorry you were going through all of that," he says. "But you can't be out acting like—"

"I don't have good sense," I say, and half laugh.

He manages a half laugh, too.

"I wasn't alone the night I broke into Stevie's," I blurt out before I lose my nerve. I want him to know everything.

"Yeah, I figured Lena had something to do with it."

"No, well, not that night. Lena was back at the beach, throwing another party, so it was just me and Craig."

The hurt I see stretching out over his face threatens to shut me up.

"I was trying to get back at you for kissing Genesis." I push my words out. "I knew how much you didn't like Craig, so I thought making out with him on *Honeypie* was the best way."

His eyes widen in shock.

"But kissing him didn't feel right. None of it did. It literally made me sick. All of it. Taking the boat out with him and Lena and Rebecca. And—"

"Wait? What?" he says, looking confused. "Y'all were sailing *Honeypie*?"

"No, it was that boat you drove the first time we went to The Cove."

"Of course," he huffs. "And how many times did y'all steal it?"

"I don't know. Not many. Maybe every night for a week or two. I can't really remember," I explain, my newfound honesty making me feel oddly optimistic.

"And that's 'not many' to you?"

"I didn't mean it like that. You don't know how many times I wanted to tell you. I was just so messed up."

"Was?"

"Yes, *was*," I insist. "Tonight reminded me of how quickly life could come to an end. That changed me."

"Please stop talking."

"Jalen—"

He gets out of the truck and heads toward my house.

I rush after him and grab his arm. "Please, Jalen. Let's get back in the truck. I can explain."

He yanks away. "I knew I smelled cologne."

"Jalen, please!"

He pauses, looks in the direction of his house, and then turns back toward me, glaring. "So, you'd come over to chill with me and then Lena would steal the keys to Stevie's when we were outside?"

"Yeah, at first," I answer, before I think to defend myself. "But they were taking the boat out before I started going with them, and I think Lena had already made a copy of the key by then."

He shakes his head rapidly, as if trying to wake himself from a bad dream. "A copy! Y'all out here making *copies?* Like it's not private property. You know Stevie's grandfather opened that shop almost a hundred years ago with canoes he built by hand? By hand, Indigo! And y'all are out here treating it with no respect!"

"I had no idea—"

"Does it matter? Did you need to know? The crazy thing is that this whole time I've been trying to keep you away from Lena when y'all are just the same. Y'all are actually perfect for each other. You only think of yourselves."

"Come on, Jalen. You know that's not true."

"Look," he says, calming down. "I'm about to go in here

and talk to your parents. But after that, don't call me, don't text me, and don't come by."

"Please Jalen," I say, following him up the steps. "If I could take everything back, I would. I'm sorry."

He opens the screen door. "Are you going to get your keys out, or do I need to ring the bell?"

"Jalen, please. I love you. You're my best friend."

"Love?" he huffs. "You can't be serious right now. You know nothing about love."

Chapter
33

"Forget Jalen," Justine says, thinking it's what I need to hear.

"I can't," I say, still crying. I haven't been able to stop since I woke her up thirty minutes ago to tell her everything.

"Didn't you always say he was goofy anyway."

I cry even harder, unable to escape the feeling that I'm the same messed-up girl I was before. I wanted to think the accident changed me, converted me into somebody else. But Jalen was right; I'm still her.

"Look, you made a mistake, or two, or ten . . . whatever," she says, and yawns.

It's early, not even six a.m. I roll over to my side. Light is starting to trickle in through the gap in my curtains, and part of me wants to get up and push them open, to let in more light. But I don't.

"You told him about the hard time you were having. You told him everything. If he still can't forgive you, then that's his problem."

"You don't get it, Justine," I sob. "He has every right to be done with me. People like me always end up pulling other people into their madness," I say, echoing Craig's words. "I'm just sad about it, okay. I've only been here two months and I've already managed to ruin my life."

"I get that you've done some terrible things. But everybody should get a pass for doing at least a few horrible things in life, as long as they don't go crazy with it."

I sniffle, wondering if I agree with her.

"Do you really think I would be friends with you if you were a bad person?"

I sniffle again.

"Remember that time that stupid Chloe girl spilled her whole bowl of veggie chili on me at lunch and you gave me your vintage Gucci sweatshirt? You wore a ratty tank top the rest of the day even though you'd just bought the sweatshirt and it was your first time wearing it. Plus, you had Miles sixth period. And on top of that, you froze your ass off for me.

They keep it, like, fifty degrees in those classrooms."

I wrap myself in the memory of my good deed until it feels like a warm hug. "Yeah, you swore she did it on purpose," I reply, reaching toward laughter but not getting there.

"She did! You know she was one of them hard-core vegetarians. And we'd *just* had a debate about eating meat in health sciences the day before! You can't tell me that was a coincidence!" Justine says, still sounding mad about it.

"Well, maybe that was one of her horrible things. I don't see you handing her any passes."

"I don't know that girl like that," she says, her voice going high. "On the other hand, you and Jalen have been tight since y'all were how old? Five? And he wants to talk about you not knowing what love is. Where is his love?"

I stare at my curtains and imagine Jalen's bright smile on the other side. Imagine him knocking on my window, calling me out of the house, to be near the lake, in the sun. Imagine my phone lighting up with his text messages, inviting me to chill with him under the moon and stars, to share dreams and cheese puffs, and start crying again.

"Look, you have less than a month before school starts. And you're gonna be the new girl. The chick all the dudes want."

I try to think of one good thing I've done for Jalen but

can only see vomit and blood. I cry even harder.

Clack, clack, clack, and the picture in my mind shifts to Justine pulling the cord to her wooden blinds and looking out at her pool. "Like I said, forget Jalen," she continues. "He'll be wishing he wasn't so hard on you come the end of August. His loss, not yours."

"But you don't understand! He's my best friend!" I say by accident.

The phone falls silent.

"I'm sorry. I—"

"You don't have to take it back just to make me feel better," she says, her voice going soft.

"See what I mean? I don't deserve you, either. I'm such a dick." I curl myself into a tight ball. The position feels hauntingly familiar, and I turn onto my back and feel tears roll down the sides of my face.

"Remember the first day of art camp, the very first time we went in the sixth grade, when you were looking for the dark-blue paint?"

"Huh?"

"Well, I had it. I wasn't even using it. I was going to paint a blue bird but decided on a purple butterfly instead."

"What are you talking about?"

"You wanted to paint a lake, and I watched you walk around the room looking for the dark blue, asking people if they'd seen it. I still had it, but I hid it in my pocket and didn't say anything."

"You were trying to steal it?"

"No, I hated how cool you were dressed and how pretty you were and how confident you seemed to be."

"But you gave me your fruit snacks at lunch."

The clanking of a spoon dropping into a bowl comes through the phone. The rattling of plastic. "I know," she says, pouring cereal. "But that was only because I felt so bad about hiding the paint. I hated myself for it. So, I decided to be your friend."

"And now you have the pleasure of me waking you up at the butt-crack of dawn with all of my problems after I've been moody and distant all summer. Not to mention me telling you—"

I stop myself. I don't want her to have to hear it again. It's not even true. Well, it is, but she's my best friend, too. Just farther away now.

"It's okay. We all do and say wrong things," she says, with her mouth full. Muted crunches come through the phone.

Filled with warmth, I say, "I love you, Justine."

A pause as she swallows. "I love you, too."

I smile at the weird goodness of sharing the words for the first time and ask her what she's eating.

She surprises me with bananas, peanuts, and milk. Tariq, the dude from the mall, put her on. They usually share a bowl on the phone together before they go to bed. Apparently, Devonte likes the new snack, too. She shoos him away from her bowl and I ask about her parents.

Her mom is thinking about opening a kolache shop, and her dad has a new remote-controlled catamaran for the pool. Apparently, it's annoying as hell.

She tells me Dani and Cara miss me, too, and I promise to group FaceTime them when I'm feeling better.

When we get off the phone, I hear my parents in the kitchen and go to them without trying to hide my puffy eyes. I see them sitting at the kitchen table, Mom sipping tea and Daddy on the phone, and remember my sadness. Remember how I lied to them the night before. The years inside me grow short and I start crying like a little girl.

Mom rushes over and pulls me into her arms. Daddy gets off the phone.

"It's okay," she says and strokes the back of my buzzed head.

"It's only a truck," Daddy assures me, joining us. "The most important thing is that you didn't get hurt."

"I felt like I was about to die," I cry into Mom's neck.

"But you're here," she whispers.

"Right here," Daddy echoes her and rubs circles on my back.

I pull away from them and sit down at the kitchen table, trying to stop myself from crying so I can say what I have to say.

They follow me, Mom sitting on my right and Daddy on my left.

"I have a lot I need to tell you."

"Go on," Mom replies gently, leaning in closer to me.

I take a deep breath and confess to drinking and driving. They yell at me about knowing better, and I try to explain how it felt to kill the deer. How it felt to see the monster's face opening to mine. To see how wrong I was about life.

Mom lays her fingers on mine, and Daddy starts rubbing my back again. Then I tell them about Jalen and Genesis. How it started with racing and playing and liking the way she styled herself. But then love and fear gave me another story.

I feel the words at work and keep going. To how I felt about moving away from my friends and school without having any say in the matter. How I feared my future. How sad it was being lost and alone in the dark.

Mom starts to cry, and I confess to wanting more of her and trying not to love her.

Daddy sighs as if he's breaking.

And then I talk about feeling guilty for not going to Gigi's funeral and being afraid of swimming in the lake. How I tried to escape into its wilderness all summer before I saw myself dead in it.

"Why didn't you tell us what you were going through? We could've helped," Mom says.

I look at her aching face and say, "I didn't know how."

"But you do now?" Daddy asks softly.

I think so, I hear inside myself, but tell them, "Yes," making my voice strong, something they can count on.

Mom looks at Daddy, and they go off to a private place in their heads. Then they are back with me, looking relieved, as if my newfound ability changes everything. For a moment it feels sweet, until my mind shifts to Jalen and a guilty, black ink spreads across my chest.

Again, my mouth is full of words—desperate, broken, hungry things. But I don't know how to calm them down and put them in the right order.

Say them anyway, I tell myself, looking down at a spot of morning light, glowing in a slanted rectangle on the wooden table.

But I don't. I push myself away from the table to get some orange juice. Push the words back on my tongue to die in my throat. But they don't. They slide down into my belly with the juice, where they slosh around and gnaw at my insides.

What She Missed

She would always be the same girl, whether she was clear to herself or others or a big question mark. Even her clarity would get lost again in the blur of life. She would forget what she had learned, make mistakes, and then remember. Only to forget again. Remember and learn, remember and learn, again and again. So she had better figure out how to forgive herself.

Chapter
34

*E*very time someone comes to sit in the beige metal foldout chair, they ruin a chance for me to get up and talk to Jalen. I know they see my annoyance—the way I force myself to fix my face before I study theirs —but I can't help it.

I'm at Homecoming, in the field on the side of the church, where I'm painting quick portraits of people. When Mrs. Williams asked me about it a few days ago, I thought it would be a chance to do something good. But I didn't realize the line would be so long and I'd be stuck off to the side under a tree painting the whole time. There probably wouldn't be so many people in line if the sun was its usual, brutal self, but it's hiding behind big, puffy clouds.

"Hello," a woman around Mom's age says, sitting down.

She has a long face with a big forehead, dark-blue eyeshadow, red lips, and thin braids tied in a side bun.

"Hi," I reply, fake smiling, staring at her multicolored beaded necklace. It reminds me of Skittles, and I start craving some.

The woman turns away from me to the podium in front of the mural, where Craig's mom is still speaking. She's talking about freedom colonies being a part of American history. About her plan to turn The Cove into a National Historic Landmark. About the fund she's setting up to help people in the community keep their land and restore the lighthouse. About investing in the preservation of blah, blah, blah.

Come on, lady, I don't have all day, I think before saying, "So you want me to paint your profile?"

"Yes, that'll be fine," she replies in a raspy voice, her attention still on Craig's mom.

Good, I think, relieved I don't have to endure another person's eyes on me for ten minutes. It makes me want to cry. Them searching me as I search them. It's too deep for me right now.

I dip my brush in black acrylic—nobody's getting color today—and draw a quick, curvy line that resembles the shape of her face. I look at the pad on the easel until I know the line looks good. Then I dip my brush again and capture the arch of her brows and eyes, the bend of her nose and chin, the roundness of her lips.

"Ain't this beautiful?" she says, turning toward me, her penciled-in eyebrows rising.

Behind her, Jalen walks out from behind the church carrying a case of water bottles. And the kids running past him in a relay race, tables of generations, the lady I'm painting, the line of descendants behind her, all fade as I watch him approach the row of coolers across the lawn, begging him to look at me.

He doesn't.

"Oh, sorry. You're trying to work," the lady says and turns her head back to its previous position.

He puts the bottles into a blue cooler and mixes them with the ice inside. When he shuts the lid and walks to throw the plastic wrapper in the trash can, I silently beg him again.

Nope.

I start drawing tiny circles around the lady's neck for her beads.

"The fact that the great-great-granddaughter of Isiah Byrd himself could do this . . . *would* do this. Let me tell you something. This is God, honey! She could be spending her money all *kinds* of different ways. Ain't no tellin' how I would be spending it if I had it," she says, and laughs.

Jalen daps up a dude I've never seen before sitting at one of the round tables near the coolers. Jalen's not wearing his hat (even though I washed it and gave it back), and I can see his face on level ten brightness. I hold back my tears by drawing a spiral for the lady's side bun.

"But to honor our ancestors . . . to preserve what they have given us," she says, voice breaking like she's going to cry.

Ashamed by how little I care, I add highlights and shadows to her face with gray watercolor.

"Alula Lake is about to be on the map, baby! You hear me? On the map!" she exclaims.

I watch Jalen walk off with the dude to go stand underneath a tree. Genesis and some other people join them, and he's at maximum brightness. Maybe a way of signaling that his life is better without me. That the bazillion text messages I've sent him the last five days proves it. That the groveling voice mail I had to call back three times to finish (because his phone kept cutting me off) was embarrassing to listen to. That the paintings of him I've left on the bed of his truck every night since the accident were horrible.

"You okay?" the woman asks.

I look at her and realize I am crying. "Sorry."

"It's emotional, isn't it?"

I nod and wipe my face. Try to forget Jalen and sign my name at the bottom of the portrait before ripping it off the pad to give to her.

"Oh, yes, baby!" she says, seeing herself. "And so quick? Girl, you got some talent!" She holds my painting up beside her face and I know she's right.

I cling to that knowledge, feeling it hint at my future, and ride it into a groove of painting the other people in line. An old man in a wheelchair, with blue rings around his eyes, beaming with pride. Twin girls wearing matching sundresses with straps tied into bows on their shoulders, so used to sharing they seem unaware that half their butts are hanging off the seat. A woman wearing a leather necklace with a gold ring hanging from it that perhaps belonged to a person she loved and lost. A tall teenage boy hunched at the shoulders. A young girl with two blond French braids, her parents standing off to the side. I wonder if they're summering here. Or maybe members of the church.

I rest my tired eyes on all of them and feel thankful. For their willingness to be my subjects. For their desire to know how I see them. The responsibility almost feels holy. Capturing their interiors and exteriors, even though we're strangers, even though I don't know what they've lived through. It begins to feel good here, with my unfamiliar friends, and I stop looking around for Jalen, begging him to forgive me.

Then Lena sits in the chair.

"Hey," I say.

"Hi." She's wearing a halter top with no bra. Usually cute, but on church grounds, the nipples sticking through the fabric seem inappropriate.

I try not to think about the last time I was with her—my hands in crushed rock, my butt in the air, fire burning the back of my head—and dip my brush in the black paint. I bring the tip toward the canvas pad but lower it because she turns her head. I raise my hand again and she does the same thing.

I decide to give her some time to settle down. "Where's Rebecca?"

"How should I know?" she says, and keeps looking around, incomprehensible.

I wonder why she waited in the long line when she clearly doesn't want to know how I see her.

"I told you that you and Jalen weren't right for each other. You should've listened," she says, her gaze finally landing on mine.

Instead of crying, I paint crooked, misaligned eyes.

"Don't take this the wrong way, but you need to stop acting so desperate. It's not cute."

I take a deep breath and draw two lines with small circles at the bottom for her nose, which I make look like it's caving in.

"At least he ended up taking your paintings out of the trash."

"He threw them away?" I ask, thinking about how I sat on the concrete floor of the studio, scrolling through all the pictures of him I took on my phone, my bottom lip repeatedly eating the snot curling over my top lip as I struggled to pick my favorite ones. Then spending five whole days and nights pouring all my hope into painting him just right.

Disgust sprouts on her face. "Look, I said he took them out, okay," she says, sounding annoyed. "You better be glad I didn't dump my spoiled tuna salad on them. I almost did."

"Gee, thanks," I say, and give her a lumpy head.

"You should probably know that he's also been dealing with his worthless mom this week. She got a new gig so she's not moving back, but she said she'd at least come for Homecoming." She fixes her gaze in the direction of the barbeque pit, and I follow it to Jalen in line talking to Craig. They're both laughing.

I do my best to rearrange the memories in my brain to match what I am seeing, but I can't.

"I told him not to get his stupid hopes up. You'd think it would be impossible to be such a bad mom. At least mine lets me come stay with her in the summer if I want to. You know, to play big sister to her two other daughters and let her porn-addicted, controlling husband lecture me about setting a better example. I'm so over it."

"I can't believe him," I say, looking at Craig, imagining him giving Jalen the blow by blow of our night on *Honeypie*.

"Tell me about it," Lena says. "It's crazy. I wasn't even allowed to be alone in the house with them. That fool convinced my mom that she needed to hire a babysitter when they went out. Meanwhile, he was so sloppy that he was out there leaving his porn pages open on the family computer in the kitchen."

I try to honor the fact that Lena is being open with me, sharing things that probably help explain why she is the way she is. I try to be sad for Jalen about his mom. But all I can think about is Craig, and why he can't just let what happened on *Honeypie* die. *Why must you keep reminding everybody and making me relive my mistakes? How about I tell everyone what the son of their benevolent savior has been up to all summer, huh?*

How about that? I ask him telepathically before asking Lena, "What did Craig tell you about the night we made out on *Honeypie?*"

"You did what!" she exclaims, like it's the best news she's ever heard. And then she lowers her voice to ask, "Does Jalen know?"

"Yeah," I answer, embarrassed that Craig is a bigger person than I am.

"Oh, is that why Jalen is so mad? I thought it was because you were wildin' out at the party. Wait, so how did he find out? Did he catch y'all in the act?" she asks, her voice rising in what sounds like hope.

"No, I told him."

"Now why would you go and do that? You know how he likes to make a big deal out of everything."

"I had to."

"You didn't *have* to do anything."

"I needed to."

She sucks her teeth. "Just like you needed to tell him about taking the boat out? Yeah, he told me. Threatened to tell Stevie and our dad if I ever did it again."

At first I wonder why she didn't go off on me when she first sat down, but then I realize she's doing her best to be a friend. Kinda touched, I say, "Well, it was fun while it lasted."

"I guess you can say the same for you and Jalen."

Her words should sting, but for some reason they don't. I can't decide if it's because I'm tired of hurting or because I can see more of who she is.

"Anyway, they're about to cut the cake. You finished?" Lena asks.

I look up and see that the people who had been waiting in line to get a portrait are gone. Everyone is walking toward a long table near the podium with huge bouquets of gold, black, and white balloons anchored to both ends.

"Almost," I say, and put a thin, black line around her neck for her choker. A tiny loop on her right nostril for her nose ring. Then I use my watercolor brush, still drenched in gray, to quickly give her portrait a little muddied color—red, green, blue, and yellow for different features. The grimy colors fight with one another and give her already distorted face a wild, dark look that weighs me down.

Glad to be done, I sign my name—Ebony Jones—with the *s* traveling off the canvas and hand it to her.

She loves it. "I can't even lie, you did your thing, Indigo."

I put the brushes in the mason jar full of water on the

ground beside my chair and start to explain, "I changed my name back to Ebony. I think I was just going through—"

"Good, there's already an Indigo at school who always sucks her tongue. You don't want to be confused with her."

By the time we make it over to the table, they're already clapping and belting out "Happy Birthday," black people style. I stand on my tiptoes to get a good look at the sheet cake, which is the size of three. It reads *155 years* in huge, black frosted letters bordered with gold.

I try to process that amount of time, but all I can think about are the dead founders.

After a few seconds, Lena knocks her elbow against mine and widens her eyes at me.

"What?"

She doesn't answer. Her lips are too busy smiling as she sings. Her body too easily swaying, her hands too happy clapping to the rhythm with everyone else. I join in and look around at all the glorious faces, all the proud and mighty hands, and think maybe the founders aren't dead at all. Maybe, even after one hundred and fifty-five years, they're still braving the wilderness to live through us.

What
She
Missed

Sitting outside at night with blackness stretching around her. Looking up at the brightest and tiniest stars. Eyeing specks of light across the lake where people live. Spotting fires. Noticing streetlights, porch lights, and headlights meandering through the hills. Seeing all of the light in the dark.

Chapter
35

I am dreaming of making black stroke after black stroke in a circle on a light black background.

"Ebony!"

I don't open my eyes. I roll over onto my back, feeling the cool pillowcase against the curve of my head, hearing rain on the roof.

"Ebony!" Mom calls again.

I try to remember the dream but can't.

Creaks in the wooden floor come closer, and then Mom is knocking at my door, opening it before I speak. "Good morning," she sings in a soft voice.

I roll over to face her.

She's still in her robe, searching me for signs of darkness.

My throat is dry, but I push out, "Morning," feeling the word sweeping away my sleepiness like a broom.

She sits down on the edge of the bed—my favorite part of the last six days, the reason I never answer her calls. "You know what we discussed. You have to get up," she says, and strokes my head.

I close my eyes and slip inside her tenderness, her smell, inside the falling rain, inside the softness of these morning minutes. It feels so good I don't want it to stop.

She gets up and I follow her down the hall, thinking about the probability that she will die before me and I will have to go to her funeral. She heads to her room to get ready for work and I watch her go until she closes the door. Then I try to scrub the thought from my brain and head to the kitchen.

Listening to Daddy singing in the shower, I get started on the oatmeal. Mom likes hers with blueberries and Daddy likes his with milk and brown sugar. I like mine with all three. Then I make Mom some green tea, Daddy some coffee, and pour myself a glass of orange juice. Scramble us all some eggs.

"Breakfast is ready!" I yell, opening the drawer to grab spoons and forks.

Daddy is out first. "Morning," he says and gives me a

hug. Then I lose him. He is far away, staring out of the window above the sink.

I lean back so that I can see what he's looking at, and there is a rainbow over the trees.

"What do you think about going to church?" he asks.

"It's Monday," I say, and start placing the silverware on Gigi's old floral cloth napkins that I've already folded and laid out.

"I know. I'm talking about starting to go regularly."

I sit down and think about the times Gigi took me to church. About nodding off during the sermon, not wanting to hold people's hands during prayers, digging through Gigi's purse for candy during the long testimonies. "I thought you and Mom always said God was everywhere."

He sits down, too. "True, but it's different going to a place to focus on God. I went, growing up, and so did your mom. We were talking about it yesterday at Homecoming. How we took it for granted . . . the spiritual foundation it gave us . . . and the friends."

"Yeah, me and Ms. Regina were praise dancers," Mom says, dropping her duffel bag against the wall next to their bedroom door. She's wearing an all-black workout set that shows a little belly.

"Really?" I say, staring at her as she sits down, trying to imagine her and her cool publicist friend as two of the teenage girls from yesterday. I felt so embarrassed watching them dance in their purple knee-length dresses and white gloves.

"I used to sing in the choir," Daddy adds.

Warmth spreads inside me as I remember everyone singing and clapping together around the cake. How happy they all looked and how I felt so . . . I don't know—safe—like I was home.

"And Mrs. Williams is planning to start on a new mural for the wall behind the pool pit," Mom says. "She'll be relying on members of the church, since school will have started and her students won't have as much free time. That'll be perfect for you."

I think about the envelope of photos Genesis gave me yesterday when I was packing up to go. Pictures of me and my rage, standing against the backdrop of the moon and stars. A hairless, foolish creature spewing venom. Then there was me drowning in my own misery after I'd fallen back into the water. I looked hideous and sad and yet somehow still beautiful.

"Thank you," I'd told her, sliding through the pictures for the second time with tears in my eyes.

"No, thank *you* . . . for letting me shoot you so . . . raw," she replied. "The photos turned out great. And they're perfect for my series. I couldn't be happier to have them."

"Yeah, I was going through it," I laughed, trying to play it off, uncomfortable with what the film might have told her about me.

"Yeah, I saw."

Seized by her honesty, I held her gaze, wanting to fill her in on everything. But the moment felt too deep for me, and I picked up the mason jar with the brushes and dumped the murky water out. "Well, my parents are waiting on me, but I'd love to return the favor and paint you. I have a garage studio. Maybe you could come over sometime."

"If you want to paint me, do it now."

"What?" I asked, confused.

"Come on. I don't have all day," she said with attitude.

Then I got that she was mimicking me, and we both busted out laughing.

At the table, I laugh out loud.

"What's so funny?" Mom asks, a little annoyed.

"No, it's just something that Genesis said yesterday."

A celebration grows on her face, and she tries to hide it by sipping her tea. "Oh, okay."

We eat the rest of our breakfast, and they hug me good-bye. Then I load the dishwasher, scrub the oatmeal pot and egg pan, wipe the counters down, sweep the floor, and take out the trash. I will do this the rest of the summer to repay my parents for the truck's new windshield—I was lucky the bull bar protected its hood and grill. Plus, I will clean the bathrooms, do the laundry, shine the wood floors, sweep the front porch, and mow the lawn. All of which I've already done earlier this week.

Now I've come to the hard part of the day. The hours when the house is empty and I've done the things I have to do and the day stretches out before me, asking what I want to do. The hours I think about going back to bed, curling up, and wasting the day away. The hours it's most tempting to break the promise I made to Justine, Cara, and Dani to stay off social. The hours when any little thing can send Jalen swirling around my brain and tears streaming down my face for so long it makes me nauseous.

I head to the studio with a plan to paint the sky and trees or a still life of Gigi's old books and ceramic pots—something simple that won't end in tears. But then I catch my reflection in the mirror against the far wall and it strikes me as a new subject. An invitation I can't refuse.

I try for hours to capture myself on the leftover canvas paper that Mrs. Williams let me keep from Homecoming, but I can't paint anything I love. And every time I try, I get hotter and more upset. I'm about to force myself to try again when it all starts feeling too familiar. So instead, I get up—golden bells outside the window ringing in the wind, applauding my choice—and head to the house, shower, eat a banana, and grab another glass of orange juice.

Back in the studio, sitting in front of the easel, I look down at my palette of browns, reds, yellows, and blues—eight different paints I mix for my skin—feeling uninspired. I get up to explore other colors on my wall of paints, but the window above is full of sun. It looks too good, and before I know it, I am chin to sky, drinking in its bright blue. It makes me miss swimming in the lake, until I imagine Gigi's dead body floating in it.

Suddenly my breath is uneasy, and I head to the table for my orange juice. I sit down on a wooden stool, take a sip, and try not to think about Gigi in the water. Then I see it in the middle of the table. The corner of the large red envelope, sticking out from my art bin like a hidden Christmas gift.

I open it. Finally. Sliding the notecard out, I recognize

the image on the front immediately. Colorful circle inside of circle in a rainbow pattern of broken brushstrokes. It's a painting by Alma W. Thomas. I try to remember its name and start to get frustrated that I can't. Then the exhibit of her work that Miles went to see on spring break in D.C. comes to me—*Everything Is Beautiful*—and it feels like enough.

I flip the card over. In his exquisitely neat handwriting, it reads:

I'm sorry. I was afraid.
We deserved a better ending.

The card, his apology, everything about it feels so sweet. I should be happy knowing that he wanted to kiss me but was too scared, that the two years we spent flirting with each other weren't all in my head. But the only thing I can think about right now is that I'm afraid, too, and don't want to be anymore.

Chapter 36

I've been standing here for ages, the sun beating down on me, tiny rocks poking the bottoms of my bare feet, daring myself to get in. I stare at the clear blue water reaching toward my toes, wondering what I'm so afraid of.

I used to fear that the lake would try to take my life, just like it took Gigi's. But I gave it plenty of opportunity to kill me this summer and it didn't. So now I think maybe I'm afraid it won't kill me. Maybe I'm afraid swimming in it will feel too good, make me feel too alive.

"Hello, lake. Hello, sun. Hello, sky. Hello, trees. We thank our God for giving us all of thee," I whisper, remembering the words Gigi made me recite at the beginning of each swim lesson.

They make me beam, until I see her dead body bobbing in the water and want to go home. I look back toward the trees, longing to escape inside their shade, inside the gentleness still hanging in the air from the rain this morning. But the wind curls in my ear and reminds me that running away will only send me in a circle that leads right back here.

I wrestle with that realization and lose. Annoyed, I dig my toes into the pebbles and turn back to the lake. Two young girls are waist deep, giggling at me. I want to assure them that even though I'm wearing a sports bra and booty shorts, and it's taking me some time to get into the water, I can still swim faster and farther than them both combined.

One dives down and does a lopsided handstand. When she pops up, ponytails dripping, the other one disappears. Hers is worse. Now they're both up, giggling at me again. I look around to see if anyone else is laughing at me, but there is only their dad, turning hot dogs on a small grill; two ladies under an umbrella, looking down at their books; and a few other people swimming, minding their business.

Still, I take off into the water—cold!—one leap after another, soles pushing against loose rocks. It would be too humiliating and disappointing to stop. I don't know how many times I've told myself that I'd never set foot in this lake again, and here I am waist deep. Amazed by the terror and beauty of it, I dive in.

Immediately I find the pebbly bottom with my palms and stack my body into a perfect handstand. Imagining the two girls looking on with their mouths open, I stretch my legs into a side split, move them into a front split, and fold them as if sitting crisscrossed—some of my favorite child-hood tricks.

When I come up, the girls are playing a splashing game, enjoying themselves too much to care.

I dive down and do it all again, this time for myself. Then I am up and swimming out toward the lighthouse, as if by muscle memory. Pulling my arms through the silky water, kicking my feet. Surprised by how easily the movements come back to me, I keep swimming until my heart is bursting and I'm out of breath.

When I look up, I'm only halfway there. I reach my toe toward the bottom, but the water is way too deep. I look to the shore, but it's too far to save me. I spin around to see if I can spot a nearby boat or Jet Ski, but they're all in the distance. Scared, I start to sink and water covers my mouth and nose.

Lie on your back and float, I tell myself, panicking, struggling to tread water.

But the picture in my head of Gigi's waterlogged body won't let me. Hating myself for being stupid enough to swim out so far, I begin to cry and thrash. Everything inside me goes dark.

But I want to live! a voice deep inside me screams.

I look out across the vast, blue water, at the lighthouse, at the thick green trees behind it, and it feels like a thousand memories of swimming in the lake, whispering the secrets that have been here for centuries about how to find your way in the wilderness.

I pray for a gathering inside of me. I summon every hurt, loss, and hideous mistake; every time I've felt jealous, stupid, angry, or ashamed; every time I was mean to Mom; every image of Gigi's dead body, of the monster, the liar who likes to tell me, *I don't care* and *I can't*; every unquenched desire; everything that I fear.

I squeeze it all close to me. Then I tip my head back and let it go.

I am remembering how to float.

Lying completely still, I look up at the bright, blue sky and watch a pair of blackbirds fly by. They disappear and I keep looking up, feeling the warmth of the sun on my body and the cool water at my back, pressing into me as I relax.

I remember floating in the lake like this when I was young, sensing my aloneness for the first time, my aliveness. I remember being in this same position when I realized there were things about myself that I didn't know.

Lying on my back now, hearing a tinkling sound as the water moves in and out of my ears, I wonder if one day the mystery will be revealed. I picture Gigi alive, swimming beside me in the lake, with all her years, and make a prediction that it will happen at age sixty-eight. *But I have no idea,* I admit, and close my eyes.

There is a sea of bright red behind my lids and tiny dots in a multitude of colors floating around. I lie still and stare at the light. Lie still and stare until the color absorbs me and I finally see how I want to paint myself.

For the background, circles inside of circles of broken brushstrokes in every shade of black I own. And for my face, a hundred different patterns—so many possibilities!—in all the colors of the rainbow.

Ideas flood in and I try to etch them into my brain, like how I want to use that indigo black paint I found in a sales bin last year for my eyes and gap, but then I relax, trusting I won't forget. This moment under the sun, on top of the lake . . . this glimpse of myself. It feels like a small miracle, and I stay still, soaking it up for as long as I can.

A cold splash smacks my upper body, and I shriek and open my eyes.

"About time!" Jalen says and laughs, his beautiful brown face beaming.

I splash him back, smiling with all the light I just witnessed behind my eyes. "Whatever! I could say the same for you!"

"You're red as hell. How long you been out here?"

"I don't even know," I reply, remembering how my nose and shoulders used to burn and peel when I went swimming without sunscreen. "Aren't you supposed to be at work?"

"Well, Kylan, this kid that usually has my nine o'clock, today got his tooth knocked out playing football with his brothers. He's only seven, so it's not a permanent tooth or anything, but he still needed to go to the dentist. Anyway, his mom could only get an appointment for this morning, so she asked if I could reschedule his lesson for this afternoon. It's been quiet at the shop, so Stevie didn't mind."

I try to pay attention to the words coming out of his mouth, but I'm overwhelmed by their randomness. It feels like everything.

"I got here early and saw your shoes on the shore, and I

was, like, *Whaat!* I couldn't believe it when I saw you out here."

"I can barely believe it myself," I say, feeling everything the way it used to be and nothing like it was.

We go quiet, treading water and searching each other with our eyes wide open. A dragonfly skims the lake between us and flies off. Then Jalen disappears underneath the water.

My heart stops for a few seconds in his absence. I'm about to go under, too, when his head pops up, closer to me.

Water dripping from his thick lashes, his face goes soft. "Look," he starts, staring me in the eyes, "I'm sorry I was so hard on you."

"It's okay. I deserved it."

"No, you didn't."

"Yes, I did."

"But you were being honest with me. I just got so mad . . . and I felt so hurt. It took me a while to process everything. But I—"

Amazed by his mercy, I dare to kiss him. He kisses me back, in the water, under the sun. His lips over my lips, my lips over his lips, a little tongue. It's sweet but short because our circling arms and legs are in the way, and I want more.

"I've wanted to do that for so long," he says, smiling.

"So why didn't you?" I ask and slip underneath the water, hoping to give him the same pang he gave me a second ago. When I pop back up, he's gone, and I'm getting tired again. Instead of spending my dwindling energy on the game we're playing, I decide to swim the rest of the way to the lighthouse.

When the lake finally gets shallow enough for my feet to meet the bed of pebbles, I arch my back and press my face up toward the watery light. Lungs gulping air, I stand up and look for Jalen across the glittering lake, hungry to feel his lips again.

Hands around my calves and I fling my face to the sun in laughter.

Hands around my waist and I'm trembling with the love between us.

His lips meet mine and I close my eyes. Color rushes in and I am full of light and memory and forever, full of everything.

Acknowledgments

For allowing me to write the books of my heart: Virginia Duncan.

For bringing a sense of calm to the business of book publishing: Jennifer Carlson.

For being the first reader of this book and my friend: Seneca Shahara Brand.

For being one of the places I discovered beauty during the pandemic and inspiring the setting of this book: Canyon Lake, Texas.

For bringing Ebony to life so beautifully on the cover: Laylie Frazier.

For raising me: Rochelle Williams and Stan Williams.

For loving me and helping me grow: Larry Animashaun.

For being a constant reminder of what's important: Amina McDyess.

For inspiring this style of acknowledgments and my writing career generally: Zadie Smith.

For reading my words: You.

Thank you. I love you.